Evolution of the Bene Israels and their Synagogues in the Konkan

Dr. Irene Judah

Evolution of the Bene Israels and their Synagogues in the Konkan

1st Edition - Published by Vishwakarma Publications in January 2017

© Dr. Irene Judah

ISBN - 978-93-85665-56-1

The views and opinions expressed in this book are the author's own and the facts are as reported by her which have been verified to the extent possible, and the publisher are not in any way liable for the same.

Published by:
Vishwakarma Publications
283, Budhawar Peth, Near City Post, Pune- 411 002.
Phone No: (020) 20261157
Email: info@vpindia.co.in Website: www.vpindia.co.in

Cover Design
Rahul Dhamane

Typeset and Layout
Gold Fish Graphics, Pune.

Dedication

I dedicate this book to my grandmother Rebecca Moses Kandlekar. She was born on March 27th 1887 and she died on 15th April 1977.

Her father was the Station Master at the Mahim station in Bombay. They lived in a spacious bungalow opposite the station. She was a tomboy in her childhood, always up to mischief, but excelled in her studies as she was a very bright and intelligent student.

She told us stories of how, when the goods trains arrived with dry fruits for the British and if the train stopped at Mahim, she would lead a gang of kids of her area to raid the train. The guards never stopped her, as she was the daughter of the station master. But if her father got to know of it, she had to face the music.

She was married at an early age as per the custom at that time, but continued to live at her father's home. She was sent to her husband's home at the age of 18 but could not tolerate the treatment meted out to her. Her spirit rebelled, she was independent minded. So she came back to her parent's home and refused to go to the in-laws home. But the parents kept on coaxing her and practically forced her. After a while she was sent back. At which point in time she got pregnant with my mother.

This time she did not go back to her husband's or her father's home but went to Pandita Ramabai's Ashram, where my mother was born. She lived there till my mother was 3 years old. She came to Bombay, put her daughter in a boarding school at that tender age, did her nursing course, where again she excelled and got two medals for excellence.

In 1918 on the 12th of November, she earned the certificate of qualification for Medical and Surgical Nursing.

On 14th May 1919, she received the Certificate of Qualification for Midwifery.

These certificates she received were from the Bombay Presidency Nursing Association which was affiliated to the University of Bombay.

Her name mentioned on the certificates is Rebeccabai Bachubai Moses. Bachubai was her pet name.

After her graduation, she worked for the Aga Khan Trust and did extremely well for herself. Her daughter i.e. my mother, Grace Hannah Moses became a doctor. She graduated from the Grant Medical College with an MBBS and DGO.

My grandmother looked after her father right through his old age until his death. He was very proud of his daughter whom he referred to as more than a son. He was also proud of his granddaughter who became a doctor. He always encouraged her to study like her mother did. My grandmother also looked after her two brothers, educated them, got them married and settled them in their lives.

She loved music and was a part of a kirtan group, where she sang and one brother played the harmonium. She was also very fond of plays and always went in a horse drawn carriage called a Victoria, which she could afford and in which she always travelled.

We granddaughters called her Nana. I salute her for everything that she did in her life. At that point in time, when things were difficult for women, she had the courage to live her life on her own terms, which is truly commendable.

My grandmother is my role model. She always encouraged us three sisters to study. I think of her every day of my life, when I salute her and thank her for everything that she has done for me. Tell her that I love her and that wherever she is, I know that she is looking out for me.

Thank you NANA.

Thank You

I thank my family for always being there for me.

Dr George Judah, my husband who always stands for me and with me like a rock. He was a Pilot in the Indian Air Force and has the typical Pilot's motto, 'do or die, no problem'. He is extremely jovial and always has a positive attitude , which is very infectious.

While in the Air Force, he did his graduation, then MBA, and registered for a PhD. He then took premature retirement from the Air Force. He joined the Symbiosis Institute of Business Management as its Director. He brought up the ranking of the institute in relation to the other institutes in India, a Glory that the institute enjoys even today. The excellent work that he has done in bringing up several institutes is so commendable that in 2015 the management of the of the Global Business School requested him to join and raise the image and standard of that institute.,at the age of 73.

Thank you George for everything, most of all for being such a wonderful husband and always being there for me.

Thank you Akiv for being such a wonderful son.

You were 5 years old when I started doing my first MD. You would come and sit on my books and tell me, enough now mummy, come and play with me. Or you would tell me to tell you a story or say, don't study I miss you. Thanks Akiv for letting mom study.

You are a real brave and courageous son; you learnt to be independent at a very early age and to do things for yourself. You never grumbled about anything, be it food or circumstances. You never demanded for toys or chocolates. You always co-operated with whatever decisions we took. Thanks a lot.

Akiv you have helped and done quite a lot of the computer jobs which I could not manage. Thanks once again.

Akiv has done mechanical engineering and an MBA with marketing and works as a manager for FMCG companies. He is married to Hannah and has a son Zohar.

Thanks Hannah for being such a wonderful daughter-in-law. You have fitted so well into my family and merged with us.

Hannah has a very cheerful personality. She is very sociable and mixes well with everyone. She is very creative, a good artist and highly imaginative. She creates such beautiful things out of scrap and throw-away materials. She has done B.Com, B.Ed and works as a primary school teacher. Thanks Hannah for just being there, and being very encouraging.

Well, last of all my grandson Zohar, who is 13 years old and has just had his Bar Mitzvah. He is a real sweetheart. We could not have asked for a better grand son, so loving, so caring and so helpful. Like his mother, he is very creative and is very good with his hands. He assembles aircrafts in no time and has won several prizes for it. He is very good at creating forms, toys and figurines out of clay. Thank you Zohar for just being there for grandma.

I love you all.

I thank Mr. Moses Penkar for taking me around in the Konkan area to all the villages wherever I asked him to. To the various Synagogues in the villages, whether they were there or not. He took me not once but six times. He knows the ins and outs of the Konkan area as he is from Pen, and also being in the RTO he is familiar with the terrain. He was extremely helpful to me, thanks once again.

Thank you Amit Menase for accompanying me on my last couple of trips and taking all the photographs and help me document them.

Lastly a big thank you to the countless people who gave me a lot of information which has been invaluable to me. It is impossible to name each one of you.

Thank You.

Foreword

CONSULATE GENERAL OF ISRAEL
MUMBAI

הקונסוליה הכללית של ישראל
מומבאי (בומביי)

David Akov
Consul General of Israel in Mumbai

In my travels across Maharashtra, I meet people who tell me about their childhood friends, neighbors or colleagues at the workplace from the Bene Israeli community, who left for Israel. Decades passed, but their Bene Israeli friends, their customs, festivals, and the ease with which the community was assimilated into the Indian culture, are remembered and cherished by the Indian people who came in contact them.

There are a few books about the Jewish community in India and their influence on local culture, cinema, institutions, and architecture, which cover the Bene Israeli community. But this is a new addition by a friend, Dr Irene Judah, Treasurer at the Succath Shelomo Synagogue at Rasta Peth, Pune. She has written this meticulously researched book, "The Evolution of the Bene Israel's and their Synagogues in the Konkan" where she takes us into the history of the Bene Israeli people, starting from the Galilee, going into details about the various possibilities about the journey, where, what, and how they came about, starting from their land of origin, to their landing on the shores of India. It takes us on a journey to find out what happened to this community over the years, their language, customs, culture, mode of dress, professions, prayers etc., why did they choose the name Bene Israel for themselves, their own names, surnames with associated causes and references, as well as their historical background over the last 2000 years upto the present Le. 2016.

In this book, Dr. Judah - who has visited many Bene-Israeli Synagogues - has covered the synagogues in the Konkan a number of times, and has documented their history and background with several anecdotes and experiences. I am sure that this book will arouse the interest of the Bene Israel community, those who have fond memories of their Bene Israeli friends, as well as those who have read or heard about the community.

David Akov

Foreword

The author of this book is known to me for over 47 years.

Nothing not even she has ever come before her Family. She has been a dedicated mother to our only son Akiv, who today, is a very Senior Executive in FMCG Company.

She, as his mother made sure that he left our home with his cup overflowing with love.

As a wife she always followed the motto 'No One, Not Even I, Before My Husband'. He reached the top most position in Management Education.

She always gave the most dispassionate advice even if it hurt the person who asked for it.

After retiring from the Armed Forces Medical College, she has written this book which was the passion of her life.

She has personally visited all the synagogues and studied each synagogue, she visited.

She gives a beautiful account of the history of the Jews and their culture.

I am sure, when you read the book you will understand the author, who is the woman I love and Adore.

Judah

Dr. George Judah

Contents

Introduction

To the outside world and even in India, it is a matter of surprise to learn that for many centuries there have been Jews settled in India and they have integrated fully in the variegated pattern of Indian life.

According to historians, there have been small communities of Jews-living in various parts of India since the tenth and eleventh century, while some say it was much earlier.

When the Romans destroyed the temple in Jerusalem, Jews residing in Judea and Northern Galilee were dispersed. Also there was the expulsion of the Jews from Spain in 1492. Since then they have acquired the reputation of being called "Wandering Jews", because, very seldom were they allowed to put down their roots. Because of their dispersion, Jews are a mixed race.

Judaism has survived through the ages because of its dynamic traditions. Jews always knew how to adapt themselves to new thoughts and new conditions. The Prophets, Moses, Yohanan Ben Zakkai and Maimonides, each of them saved Judaism at different points in time, at its hour of crisis, by adjusting to the prevalent situation. The entire Talmud is essentially a reinterpretation of the earlier Judaism of the Bible to meet the problems of a new age. Even post Talmudic Judaism continued this process of growth and development.

Judaism is the complete culture and civilization of the Jewish people. It possesses all the attributes of language, literature, art, music, customs, laws, institutions and history.

The Jewish nation has survived the downfall of its own nation. This above all, is due to the genius of Rabbi Yohanan Ben Zakkai, who turned religious study into a new form, in which the national existence of the Jews found expression, so, besides the history of nearly two thousand years of suffering and wandering, we can take pride of an equally extensive history of intellectual effort. Studying and wandering, thinking and enduring, learning and suffering filled this long period. Thinking has become a characteristic trait of the Jews as suffering is, or to be more exact, it has been called "thinking rendered suffering". It was our thinkers who prevented the wandering nation, this true "Wandering Jew" from sinking to the level of brutalized vagrants or vagabond gypsies.

Since then, they have become international; they have dispersed throughout the world. Whenever and wherever allowed, they have become nationals of the countries of their residence. The Bene Israels were one such group who have put down their roots in India, although they were not the only group here.

The first mention of Jews in connection with India is found in the book of Esther which dates back around second BC. Mention is made of the decrees of the Persian Monarch Xerxes (Ahasverosh in the Bible), relating to the dispersion of the Jews throughout the 127 provinces of his empire, stretching from India to Baluchistan which was then a part of India, but now it is partly in Pakistan and partly in Iran.

It is quite likely then, that there were Jews in India, but none of those are known to have survived or even if they did survive, there is nothing further documented about them.

The mystery of the lost ten tribes, dispersed and considered vanished nearly 3000 years ago, has baffled historians for centuries. Scholars and historians have made attempts from time to time to piece together biblical and historical records and documents in several languages, as well as archeological discoveries in various countries to trace their whereabouts.

The dispersal of the Lost Ten Tribes was and is viewed with great concern by the Jews and also many travelers who came up with stories concerning the tribes they met in the most unbelievable circumstances in various parts of the world.

It has been mentioned by historians that some members of the tribe of Asher and Zebulon, participated in shipbuilding and sea faring activities together with the coastal people in the Konkan area.

Mention about Jews permanently settled in India was found in a letter written by a Danish Christian missionary J.A. Sartorius, who on hearsay evidence, mentions about a community of Jews in Surat and Rajapore in Gujarat, who call themselves Bene Israels, who do not have the Bible or know Hebrew and the sole formula of prayer or a religious doctrine is the word "SHEMA" (Hebrew for HEAR).

After J.A. Sartorius, another historian Ezekiel Rahabi wrote that there were Jews in India at Vijapur and they are also scattered in all the towns of the Marathas. He wrote a letter in 1768 where in he mentioned that prior to 1768, a few Bene Israels sought guidance from Cochini Jews. He also mentions that one Bene Israel studied in Cochin for 4 years.

About 2000 years ago, a century after the destruction of the second temple, a historian who travelled to India on a Roman ship, recorded that in one of the Indian ports, he met a small community of Jews who observed the Sabbath strictly and refused to sell food to the Roman sailors on that day.

Several centuries later, Moses Maimonides, mentioned in one of his letters to the Rabbis of Lunel France, that so far as he knew, there were Jews in India who observed the Sabbath, circumcised their male offspring on the eighth day after birth, though they did not have any sacred books, not even the Torah but only had the oral tradition to guide them.

The British knew that there were Jews who had already integrated into the Indian social fabric in the Kokan and Malabar coasts. David Gilmour, a knighted historian in his biography of Lord George Curzon, wrote that the prevalent feeling amongst the British at that point in time was to route all Jews to India, as they have a history of assimilating every Jew as their own.

A well known Christian historian, maintained that there were Jews settled in both the Konkan and Malabar regions, who had settled much before their arrival in 50 AD. Although they were Jews themselves, their mission was to evangelize the Jews of India. (Christianity had not yet been established, which happened 330 years after the death of Christ whose actual name was Yehoshua Ben Yacov.) They were directed to the Jewish settlements. They knew that these Jews were the first to come, not only as traders but also as settlers.

Two apostles, as they subsequently came to be known as, came to India to preach Christ's teachings. Once Christianity was established, one was referred to as St. Thomas who went to Malabar and to whom is attributed the origin of the Syrian Christians. The other apostle later referred to as St. Barthelmo, preached and converted people in the area not far from where the Bene Israels had landed. The historians categorically state, that they were directed towards the Jewish settlements. However, very few Bene Israels were converted to Christianity.

Several hundred years after the advent of the Bene Israels and the Cochinis on the soil of India, a steadily growing stream of Jews began to arrive and settle down in this country. They came from the middle east and later from the persecution ravaged countries of Europe. The main reason besides persecution that brought these communities to India was commercial.

❑ ❑ ❑

Bene Israel's their Beginnings
in the Konkan

The Bene Israel community has a most interesting origin and past, which makes them one of the most remarkable historical and cultural people in India if not in the world. They arrived more than 2000 years ago. They journeyed to India not only for commercial purposes, but also to escape the turmoil and tumult which were common features of that time, around the land of Palestine. Scholars and historians are in conflict over the exact date of their arrival in India. One historian Dr Wilson, in an address to the Bombay branch of the Royal Asiatic Society in 1838, expressed the view that the Bene Israels belong to the lost Ten Tribes of Israel.

The Bene Israels, a small ancient community settled on the west coast of Maharashtra, have a long history of survival. It is a miracle that, though remote from mainstream Judaism, they have maintained their traditions through the centuries. They are indeed part of the lost tribes.

Historical evidence which is available, states that the ancestors of the Bene Israels, fled from Northern Galilee during the persecution instituted by foreign enemies, chief amongst them Antiochus Epiphanes who invaded the land around 175 BC, and which had finally lead to the Maccabian Revolt and Uprising. History has recorded that Antiochus Epiphanes in 175 BC planned to exterminate the religion of the Hebrews. He killed 40,000 Jews in just 30 days, sold a similar number as slaves, took some thousands as slaves for himself, defiled their temple, pillaged their treasure and collected a large bounty for himself. However, in spite of that, some Jews did manage to escape.

The flight of the Bene Israels occurred before the Maccabian uprising. This is based on the religious observances of various holidays, fasts, birth, marriage, burial and sacrificial rites that the Bene Israels observed. They did not celebrate Hanukah, which commemorates the incident after the Maccabees liberated the temple. Also the Bene Israels were not aware of the destruction of the second temple by Titus.

Thus began the journey of the Bene Israels, travelling the routes opened by King Solomon for trade with India and other countries of the east. This small group of fleeing Jews in boats, reached or rather got shipwrecked on the western coast of India, in the Konkan region about 15 miles from Cheul. The Cheul creek is between Bassein and Mahad creek. Cheul was the chief port of trade in 2 BC.

This theory gains credence, because Cheul was a flourishing trade centre at that time. Their destination was Cheul, but while in the Cheul creek, their ships were caught in a storm and they were shipwrecked near the Henery Kenery islands.

The shipwreck was either due to a storm or their ignorance of navigation along the Konkan coast, which is treacherous and very rocky.

The total number of Jews who were shipwrecked is not known, nor the number of boats in which they were travelling. What is clearly known is that 14 people, 7 men and 7 women of the group survived. Also it is not known nor documented, how only 7 men and 7 women of the group survived. Also, it is not known how only 7 men and 7 women and not any other odd number survived, seems miraculous though odd. Also it is not known whether these 7 men and 7 women were husband and wife, and if so how many of the couples were really couples.

When they landed in Nawgaon, they were lying unconscious on the beach. Local fisher folk gave them resuscitation, took them to their residences, fed them and made them strong. In other words, helped them in every possible way. Further, they helped them settle in Nawgaon and later on as their numbers increased, helped them settle in the neighboring villages and helped them support themselves. Oil pressing, coconut and betel nut farming, animal husbandry and carpentry became their professions.

The survivors took refuge in the village of Nawgaon, where they buried their dead co-travelers and that spot is there till today, though not clearly marked but is visible, sort of, as mounds of stone. A memorial has been built there to commemorate this event.

Above is the photograph of the mounds
where the ancestors were buried.

❏ ❏ ❏

Where Did they Come From?

The ancestors of the Bene Israels came directly from Palestine 175 years before the Christian Era (CE). If the ancestors of the Bene Israels came to India from Yemen or any other place 2000 years ago, they would have given up the practice of sacrificial meat offerings, as was done by Jews elsewhere, after the destruction of the second Temple. The Jews who left after the destruction of the second Temple and those who left previously, migrating to other lands, but on receiving the news of the destruction, stopped this practice.

Also, Jews who had been lead into captivity at the time of destruction of the first Temple and did not return for 70 years or more had already forsaken this custom and practice.

But amongst the Bene Israels, this custom is still in vogue, which indicates that, they were still in Palestine during the existence of the second Temple. They probably left before its destruction i.e. about 2000 years ago. Today, offerings are in the form of a dish (cooked food) offered in God's name or a chicken is cut, but there is no burning, as they do not have any alter for that purpose. After the circumcision or just before house warming prayers, a chicken is cut as a form of sacrifice. The offerings are also as a thanksgiving, after recovery from a severe illness as directed by the Levitical code.

The offerings make it obvious that the ancestors of the Bene Israels must have been in Palestine where these offerings were in vogue.

Had it not been for the women who survived the shipwreck, all the various fasts and feasts, rites and ceremonies, manners and customs, could never have been observed and kept intact for the future generations, as they have been. The rites and ceremonies which they observed are the same as described in the Torah and do not differ from those observed by other Jews in the middle east.

The ancestors of the Bene Israels must have been well off when they left their homeland, because they must have had to either buy or charter ships for their voyage or pay for their passage. They must have been forced to leave because of the imminent danger to their lives and properties and to leave it all in a hurry.

The Bene Israels began their life in India with a variety of complexes and considerations. They were apprehensive of strangers, unsure of their surroundings, having borne deep scars of a savage persecution in the lands from where they had fled. They entered their new homes with a prayer for the best and preparation for the worst.

The Bene Israels had the habit of remaining in obscurity, which had become their second nature. Also, the Konkan area where they first settled was inhabited by less educated Hindus, so there was no intellectual progress and they probably forgot what little knowledge they had brought with them.

Considering that only 7 men and 7 women survived the shipwreck and after nearly 2000 years of living in India, it was observed that their numbers were never more than 10,000 at any given point in time, especially in the earlier years. This was probably because they may have had to endure famine, destitution, epidemics like cholera, small pox, plague etc, which would have further decreased their numbers. Also their houses must have been constantly pillaged and burnt by robber tribes such as the Pindaries. Most importantly, the areas had frequent petty wars and skirmishes; so many Bene Israels may have lost their lives in these skirmishes. Subsequent census reports in the later part of the 1900's do show higher numbers.

The language that the ancestors of the Bene Israels spoke was the language of the land they fled from, was it Hebrew or was it Aramaic or??? This over a period of time, they lost out on, adopting the language of the locals i.e. Marathi. This process must have taken several centuries.

The Bene Israels dispersed along the Konkan coast, to places such as Roha, Nowgaon, Mahad, Rajapuri, Kihim, Shrivardhan, Mhasla, Revdanda, Thal, Akshi, Nagoan, Saswane, Dighordy, Nawgoan and many others. Much later, again for economic reasons, they settled in Bombay (now Mumbai), Poona (now Pune), Ahmedabad, Karachi, Rangoon (now Myanmar), Igatpuri, Bhor and Satara. Also, small groups settled in Ajmer in Rajasthan, Indore, Jabalpur in Madhya Pradesh, Belgaum in Karnataka, Nagpur, Delhi and elsewhere, wherever jobs took them, where they prospered and built synagogues and adopted the local languages for conversations.

Being Jewish in India means understanding how they got here. They descended from a group of wanderers who were shipwrecked while travelling and even after the shipwreck, they kept the necessary tenets (criteria) of Judaism, namely Kashruth, Circumcision, Sabbath, and Shema. The significance being that, even after the shipwreck, they maintained their Jewishness when all else was lost.

The Jewish community in India, understands these sentiments more than any other Jewish community in the Diaspora. They understand strong and unique Judaism of the wandering people.

The coastal region was where they settled and took to oil pressing and agriculture, including coconut and betel nut plantations. Why they took to oil pressing, there are two explanations given by historians. One is that – they brought the knowledge and art of oil pressing of olives, from their homeland and found it easy to continue in the same trade. Thus, they worked for 6 days and rested on the 7th day. So, their neighbors called them Shanivar Tellis i.e. Saturday oil pressers, as they did not press oil on Saturday as enjoined in the mosaic laws.

Photograph of an Oil pressing machine taken in 1985s. The only one existing in the Konkan region, in the village of Nandgaon at the residence of the Cheulkar family. Bullocks were used to crush out the oil by making them go round and round so as to turn the wheels and squeeze out the oil.

The second explanation as to the vocation of oil pressing as a means of livelihood, was their numbers, which was miniscule in the beginning and they were very concerned about their safety and security, especially of their women, all of whom, as reports have it, were extremely beautiful. They thought the best way to ensure their safety would be to place them beyond the reach of violators, by attaching to themselves the stigma of untouchability, which was prevalent in the country they settled in. The settlers chose to work as oil pressers because in India, that was the vocation of the lowest caste i.e. the untouchables. The caste system was very much prevalent in those times, although it exists even today in certain areas.

Though subjected to a rapid process of Indianization, they retained enough of their former religious instincts and knowledge to labor for 6 days of the week and rest with total abstinence from work on the 7th day, i. e. Shabbath.

The Bene Israel ancestors began their life in India under tragic circumstances and disadvantages. It is possible that persecution and the policy of extermination drove them out of the lands of their fore fathers and they must have carried with them the holy scrolls containing the laws and tenets of Judaism, which got lost in the shipwreck. This could have been one possibility.

Another possibility was that the Bene Israels, when they lived in Persia possibly, their religious laws were transmitted orally and were observed as the laws mentioned in the Torah. But after their ordeal and the shipwreck, the elders who were the bearers of the oral traditions were no more or they did not pass on the oral traditions to the subsequent generations due to various reasons and who in turn over a period of time no longer remembered them.

They only retained the custom of circumcision and the observance of Yom Kippur, which they did diligently. They observed the Yom Kippur fast on the exact day and how they managed to do that, I could not find out. Since they came to India, on Yom Kippur day, they would close themselves in their homes from sunset on Erev Kippur after an early meal and the whole of the next day, without speaking a word to anyone. Each one would sit and remain silent, as if in meditation. They broke their fast only after sunset. They did not have the prayers books and the prayers that they knew by oral tradition were forgotten after their misfortunes.

The question often put forth was that, "Are they Jews or Israelites?"

The Bene Israels admit that for their religious observances and practices, they had to be instructed by the Arabian and Cochini Jews. The very fact that they needed to be instructed by them in the religious customs and observances which were being observed by Jews all over the world, forms the main basis of the presumption that they have been established for ages in this country and belong to the exiled and lost Ten Tribes of Israel.

According to Dr Claudius Buchanan, who, when he was making inquiries about the lost Ten Tribes, found that large a number of Israelites were in Chaldea, a few families migrated to regions as remote as Cochin and Rajapur in India. The last mentioned place is in the district bordering Nagotne creek, where many Bene Israels had settled.

The want of a Sefer Torah or a book of the Law, placed them in a situation in which no other congregation of the world was in. The significance of the designation Jew, the emphasis on they being called as Bene Israels, a name which they chose for themselves, was really relevant. Amongst them, there was a preference for the name Reuben and not Judah or Esther, all of this indicating that they were from the lost Ten Tribes and that they were indeed God's chosen people. This provides strong circumstantial evidence, that they are indeed Israelites, who were remnant of the tribes who were dislodged from their homes by the Assyrian Kings.

Solomon Reineman stated that the Bene Israels were exiled from their land by Shalmanezzar, the Assyrian King, before the destruction of the first Temple. They settled in Persia and did not return when the second Temple was built. In 612 when Ali Ibn Aby Talib conquered Persia and took over all the lands, he forced the Bene Israels to convert to Islam and ruled over them with a sword. All those who could, escaped, which included both the Bene Israels and the Parsis.

First, they went to Abu Shahar and stayed there for 20 years. They built boats and ferries for themselves so they could cross over to East India, because they had heard that the Indians were mainly Hindus, who would not persecute or convert them. After the Jews and the Parsis completed their work on the boats, they set sail for India. When they were 5 miles off the coast, they were shipwrecked.

It is also believed that because of their miniscule numbers, in time, the men folk took local women as wives but on one condition that they follow the faith of their husbands and be referred to as Bene Israels. Initially, they took non Jewish wives. When they multiplied and their numbers increased, they were careful of inter-caste marriages. But I doubt this was ever successful, as there have been inter-caste marriages then and even now. I doubt it ever stopped. Intercaste marriages with the local inhabitants accounts for the physical resemblance to their neighbors.

There was a change in their lifestyle. Also, the environment, weather conditions, food, mode of eating, conditions of living, type of houses and many other different factors which were involved, modified their complexions and physical appearance. Their fair complexion gradually changed to a darker shade. They adopted the local mode of dress to merge with the locals.

As mentioned earlier, once in India and over a period of time, maybe several years or probably even hundreds of years and possibly under the stress and strain of the new and hard life which they were struggling to adapt to, they forgot the main portions of the prayers and religious services.

But they never forgot the Shema—"Hear O Israel the Lord our God, the lord is One". These all-important words were their only link with their religious past. They were most certainly aware of the significance of the Shema. They knew that the Shema is the most important prayer in Jewish history. With the Shema on their lips, martyrs of every age, including our own, have died for the sanctification of God's name and the glory of Israel. Its words are the very last spoken by every Jew and its sacred syllables the first taught to little children. It is the central feature of the morning and evening service and is recited before retiring at night and waking up in the morning.

The Bene Israels were aware of the importance that Shema holds in Jewish law and the sentiments associated with it. It played an important role in the service of the second temple and is probably the oldest part of the liturgy.

They were also aware that the Shema, which opens with the clarion call, "Hear O Israel The Lord Our God, The Lord Is One", an avowal of Israel's uncompromising belief in the absolute unity of God, the basis of the faith in the universal brotherhood of man and proclaiming our allegiance to God.

The Bene Israels were also aware that the unity of God, love for him and loyalty to his kingdom, duty of educating our children in the study of the Torah, the principle of retribution and the importance of rituals, all these fundamentals are indicated in 3 short paragraphs of the Shema - Ve'ahavta, Vehaya and Vayomer. No wonder that Jewish tradition declares that, "He who recites the Shema with true inwardness of spirit is as though he had fulfilled all the Commandments of the Torah".

The two words Bene Israel, which means Children of God, are commonly mentioned in the Old Testament. How and why they choose this name for themselves? As the story goes, after the death of King Solomon, the Jewish nation was divided into two kingdoms; one was Israel while the other Judah. The former comprised the Ten Tribes while the latter, the remaining two, Benjamin and Judah, which occupied the southern part of Palestine. When Jerusalem was besieged and taken over by King Nebuchhadnezzar, a large number of Jews, from the tribe of Judah were led away as captives to Babylon. Gradually these exiles took up the position of colonists rather than captives. Lands were allotted to them and they grew to own and love the soil they cultivated. But within themselves they kept the knowledge that though now they were Babylonians and not Palestinians, they belonged to the tribe of Judah.

Hence the name Judean or Jew came into being, which is now applied to the "Scattered Race" all over the world. The word Jew is of a later origin than Israel. The former is derived from the word Judah, while the latter Israel to the ten tribes, carried into captivity when Palestine was invaded by Shalmanesar, about 130 years before the fall of Jerusalem and were dispersed to other regions. Consequently our ancestors adopted for themselves the name Bene Israel, which means sons of Israel, because they were unable to prove their lineage from the tribe of Judah, because they had possibly lost all their historical records in the shipwreck.

Also at that point in time, our ancestors adopted the name Bene Israel, as Mohamedan power prevailed in India and Islam was propagated by the sword. Hatred for the name Yehudi (Jew) was a ground for being compelled to renounce their religion or lose their lives and property. They thought it wise to adopt the less hated name Bene Israel, which served both purposes, retention of their ancient name and faith and preservation of their lives and property.

The Bene Israels remember a David Rahabi, probably an Egyptian, who suddenly appeared in their midst, about the year 1000 AD according to some, while according to others 1400 AD and still some others, 1600 AD. He ascertained their Jewishness by observing their traditions.

Also to ascertain their knowledge of the dietary laws, Rahabi bought a basketful of fish, both with scales and fins and some without, to be cooked for him. He observed that the women promptly separated the fish with scales and fins for cooking and discarded the rest.

Rahabi was fully convinced about their Jewishness. He organized Hebrew teaching classes for them and taught them the tenets of Judaism. Besides, he also organized classes for observance of religious rites which they had probably forgotten. He appointed three Kazis (means teachers in Urdu) from among the ones he had trained, one a Jhiradkar, one a Shapurkar and one a Rajpurkar to function as teachers and conduct religious services and rites. Also, that they should teach the rest of the Bene Israels, which they did religiously and zealously.

Unfortunately his personal teaching did not last for long – how long exactly is also not known. A village chieftain killed him, why ---reason?? –Out of?? His grave is present in the village of Sarul near Alibagh. The wordings on the gravestone are not legible, nor is his name. However locals point out his grave. David Rahabi was the main person responsible for bringing modern Judaism to the Bene

Israels. It was during the time of David Rahabi, that the Ketuba (marriage bond) was introduced.

After his death, the Bene Israel's continued to live, pray and worship in the light of his guidance. The extent to which they adhered to their religion is evident from their religious observances and later on to the large number of synagogues that they built throughout the Konkan, the rest of Maharashtra and also other places in the rest of India, especially during the last few centuries. The Bene Israels are considered to be one of the most devout people in the world. The credit goes to David Rahabi, unfortunately whose exact date of arrival and death in the Konkan is not known.

❑ ❑ ❑

Names and Surnames of the Bene Israel's

There is a belief amongst the Bene Israels that from our ancestors come our names, from our virtues comes our honor.

The concept is that the Bene Israels got their names from the villages where they resided, which according to some historians is not so. Thus the origin of their names is a disputable point.

According to some historians, the earliest settlers spoke Hebrew and the land that they came from was most probably Yemen, Persia or Spain, where they were farmers. Now the Hebrew word for farmer is Kar or Fkar or Kfar and if the person's name was Tal the surname became Talkar, as was the custom even in Europe and elsewhere, where the surname was the name of the person along with his profession. So Tal the farmer became Talkar, which became his surname. This mode is similar to the mode in the scriptures too. For example, Elijah the prophet's surname was Tishbite from Tishbi, a town in Napthali. Cochini Jews have also taken their surnames from the localities of their residence, for example Halegoa, Rahabi, Mizrahi and so on.

Still other historians believe that as per the local custom prevalent in the Konkan, the Bene Israels took their surnames from the names of the villages where they lived and added kar to it. There are more than 350 surnames that been found with the corresponding villages in the Konkan area. I have collected 325 surnames, which I have been collecting since my childhood, and I have put them in alphabetical order, with the corresponding name of the village wherever possible.

A		
Sr. No.	**Surname**	**Village**
1	Adharnekar	Adharne
2	Agarwarkar	Agarwada
3	Akshikar	Akshi
4	Alibaghkar	Alibagh
5	Ashtivkar	Akshi
6	Ampurkar	Ambepur
7	Ambepurkar	Ambepur
8	Aptekar	Apta
9	Ashtamkar	Ashtami
10	Ashtikar	Ashti
11	Astivkar	Astive
12	Ashtekar	Ashte
13	Asrekar	Asre
14	Avdekar	Avde
15	Avedkar	-
16	Awaskar	Awas
17	Awtankar	Awtane

B		
Sr. No.	**Surname**	**Village**
1	Badrekar	Badre
2	Bamanolkar	Bamnoli

3	Bandarkar	Bandar
4	Bankar	Banke
5	Barsulkar	Barshul Barshiv
6	Barazkar	Baraz
7	Belkar	Belkhar Belkade
8	Belgaonkar	Bedgaon
9	Belulkar	Beluwadi
10	Bhastekar	Bhaste Bhatsai
11	Bhachekar	Bhaste
12	Bhalgaonkar	Bhalagaon
13	Bhalkar	Bhal
14	Bharjekar	Bharje
15	Bhinjekar	Bhinje
16	Bhinjikar	Bhinjigaon
17	Bhorankar	Bhoran
18	Bhorapkar	Bhorap
19	Bhorupkar	Ghera Sudhagad
20	Bhonkar	Bhongaon
21	Bilakar	Bilagoan
22	Birwadkar	Birwadi
23	Borgavkar	Borgaon
24	Borgaonkar	Borgaon Khurd Borgaon Budruk
25	Borgharkar	Borghar
26	Borlekar	Borli
27	Borlaikar	Borli

C		
Sr. No.	**Surname**	**Village**
1	Chanerkar	Chaner
2	Changaonkar	Changaon
3	Chandgaonkar	Chandgaon
4	Chandrolkar	Chandor Chandorkar
5	Charikar	Chari
6	Cheulkar	Cheul
7	Chincholkar	Chincholi Chinchoti Chinchawali
8	Chordekar	Chorde
9	Corlekar	Corle
10	Corleykar	Corley

D		
Sr. No.	**Surname**	**Village**
1	Damkhedkar	Damkhed
2	Dandekar	Dande Nandgaon
3	Dandoolkar	Dandguri
4	Dandulkar	Dandgulkar
5	Dandgolkar	Dandgol
6	Deulkar	Devali
7	Dewkar	Dew
8	Dhatavkar	Dhatav
9	Dhatawadkar	Dhatawadi
10	Dhokarkar	Dhokawade
11	Dighorkar	Dighati Dighodkar
12	Divekar	Dive

13	Doodkar	-
14	Doodhkar	Dudkar
15	Dolwalkar	Dolwal
16	Dootkar	-
17	Dusvikar	Dushmi Khar Pada

E		
Sr. No.	Surname	Village
1	Erulkar	Yeral

F		
Sr. No.	Surname	Village
1	Fansapurkar	Fansapur
2	Finjekar	Finje

G		
Sr. No.	Surname	Village
1	Gadapkar	Gadapkari
2	Galsoorkar	Garsool
3	Gamarlekar	Gamarle
4	Garapkar	-
5	Gadkar	Gadkari Garsulkar
6	Galsurkar	Galsure Galsulkar
7	Ghanekar	Parhar Shrigaon
8	Gartzurkar	Garzur
9	Ghosalkar	Ghosale
10	Ghoralekar	Ghorale
11	Ghorapkar	Ghorap

12	Gordekar	Gorde
13	Gowalwadkar	Gowalwadi
14	Gordekar	Gorde

H		
Sr. No.	**Surname**	**Village**
1	Halbekar	Halbe
2	Hardikar	Hardi
3	Haramkar	Haram
4	Haramkekar	Haramke
5	Hazrasholkar	Hazrashol

I		
Sr. No.	**Surname**	**Village**
1	Indapurkar	Indapur
2	Ivalekar	Ivale
3	Ivlekar	Ivle

J		
Sr. No.	**Surname**	**Village**
1	Jawalikar	Jawali
2	Jhiradkar	Jhirad
3	Jitekar	Jite
4	Jeetekar	Jeete

K		
Sr. No.	**Surname**	**Village**
1	Kamarlekar	Kamarli
2	Kamarkar	Kamare

3	Kandlekar	Kandli
		Kandale
		Kandal
4	Kandli	Kandal
5	Kandlakar	Kandla
6	Kanenkar	Kanen
7	Kanehkar	Kaneh
8	Kanhekar	Devakanhe
9	Karnenkar	Karnen
10	Karlekar	Karle
11	Kasukar	Kasu
12	Kasookar	Kasu
13	Kehimkar	Kihim
14	Khajawkar	Khajaw
15	Khamgaonkar	Khamgaon
16	Khamkar	Khamb
17	Khanavkar	Khandala
		Khanav
		Khanaw
18	Khandalkar	Khandal
19	Kharilkar	Khar Karavi
20	Kharulkar	Kharul
21	Khanvilkar	Kharavali
22	Khanavkar	Khanavli
23	Khandlekar	Khandle
24	Khandekar	Khande
25	Khandalkar	Khande
26	Khorkar	Khorki
27	Khulabkar	Kolaba
28	Khulapkar	Kolaba
29	Khursaikar	Khursai

30	Khurraikar	Khurrai
31	Killekar	Kille
32	Kokbankar	Kokban
33	Kolabkar	Kolaba
34	Kolatkar	Kolad
35	Koladkar	Kolad
36	Koletkar	Koleti
37	Koltukar	-
38	Korlekar	Korlai
39	Kordekar	Kordai
40	Koltukar	Koltuk
41	Kulabkar	-
42	Kurekar	Kude
43	Kurgaonkar	Kudgaon
44	Kurulkar	Kurul

L
None that I could find

M		
Sr. No.	**Surname**	**Village**
1	Malekar	Male
2	Malheghkar	Maleghar
3	Malyankar	Malyan
4	Malinkar	-
5	Mangaonkar	Mangaon
6	Mangaon	Budruk
7	Mangaon	Khurd
8	Mankar	Mann Jhirad
9	Mapgaonkar	Mapgaon
10	Mabgaonkar	Mapgaon

11	Massil	-
12	Mazgaonkar	Mazgaon Majgaon
13	Mazgavkar	Mazgav
14	Mazronkar	-
15	Mendrekar	Mendre
16	Medhekar	Medhe
17	Mhacuakar	-
18	Mhedekar	Mhede
19	Mhashilkar	Mhasla
20	Mhaslekar	Mhasle
21	Mhasilkar	Mhasla
22	Mhaisabkar	Mhaisab
23	Mhaisapkar	Mhaisap
24	Mhashilkar	Mhashil
25	Mhashulkar	Mhashule
26	Mhedekar	Mhede
27	Morbekar	Morbe Morba
28	Mordrekar	Mordre
29	Mulekar	Mule
30	Murudkar	Murud

N		
Sr. No.	Surname	Village
1	Nagavkar	Nagaon
2	Nagawkar	Nagaon
3	Nagokar	Nagone
4	Nagotkar	Nagotne
5	Nagotnekar	Nagotne
6	Nandgaonkar	Nandgaon

7	Navgaonkar	Navgaon
8	Navgharkar	Navghar
9	Nagothnekar	Nagothn
10	Naugokar	Naugoke
11	Navgharkar	Navghar
12	Nawgharkar	Nawghar
13	Nawgavkar	Nawghar
14	Nigadkar	Nigade Nigadi
15	Nigrekar	Nigade
16	Ningrekar	Nigade Nowbaskar
17	Nowgaonkar	Nowgaon
18	Nowsherkar	Nowsher
19	Nowbaskar	-

O		
Sr. No.	**Surname**	**Village**
1	Omerdekar	Omerde
2	Oomerdekar	Omerde

P		
Sr. No.	**Surname**	**Village**
1	Pabrekar	Pabre
2	Palkar	Pali
3	Pali	Budruk
4	Pali	Khurd
5	Paralikar	Parali
6	Parankar	Paran
7	Parulkar	Parul
8	Penkar	Pen

9	Pezarkar	Pezari
10	Phansapurkar	-
11	Pingle	Pingalsai Budruk
12	Pingalsai	Khurd
13	Poynadkar	Poynad
14	Puikar	Pui
15	Pugavkar	Pugaon

Q
None that I could find

R		
Sr. No.	**Surname**	**Village**
1	Ramrajkar	Ramraj
2	Ramrazkar	Ramraz
3	Rajpurkar	Rajpuri
4	Raspurkar	Raspuripur
5	Razpurkar	Raz
6	Raikar	Raiwadi
7	Rajpurikar	Rajpuri
8	Revdandekar	Revdanda
9	Rohekar	Roha
10	Ruikar	Rui

S		
Sr. No.	**Surname**	**Village**
1	Sabaskar	Shahabag
2	Sagaonkar	Sagaon
3	Saigaonkar	Saigaon
4	Saigavkar	Saigav

5	Saikar	Saiwadi
6	Sakshikar	Sakshi
7	Salavkar	Salav
8	Salsettekar	Salsette
9	Sankar	Sahan
10	Saralkar	Saral
11	Saroolkar	Sarool
12	Sarsolikar	Sarsoli
13	Sassoonkar	Sasavne
14	Satamkar	Satambe
15	Satarkar	Satare
16	Shapurkar	Shapur
17	Shahapurkar	Shahapur
18	Shirgaoonkar	Walke
19	Shirgavkar	Shirgaon
20	Shirkolkar	Shirkol
21	Shirsekar	Shirse
22	Shriwardhankar	Shriwardhan
23	Shivardhankar	Shivandhar
24	Sogavkar	Sogaon
25	Sogaonkar	Sogaon
26	Songavkar	Songaon
27	Songaonkar	Songaon
28	Songaoson	Songaon

T		
Sr. No.	Surname	Village
1	Tadgaonkar	Tadgaon
2	Talegaonkar	Talegaon
3	Talegaon	Goregaon

4	Talekar	Tala
5	Talhekar	Talekhar Tala
6	Talkar	Tala Talekhar Tale
7	Tarne	Tale
8	Tarankhopkar	Tarankhop
9	Telulkar	Telul and Talauli
10	Thalkar	Thal
11	Thulkar	Thul
12	Thugkar	Thug

U		
Sr. No.	**Surname**	**Village**
1	Umerdekar	Umbarde
2	Ursolikar	Ursoli

V		
Sr. No.	**Surname**	**Village**
1	Vadgaonkar	Vadgaon
2	Vadhavkar	Vadhav Budruk
3	Vadavkar	Vadav
4	Vakrulkar	Vakrul
5	Valvatkar	Valve
6	Valakkar	Valak
7	Valakar	Valak
8	Varkar	Varke
9	Varkhanjenekar	Varkhanje
10	Varhadkar	Varhad
11	Varvanjenekar	Varvanje

12	Varulkar	Varul
13	Varvatnekar	Varvatne
14	Varsulkar	Varsoli
15	Varvanjenekar	Varvanje
16	Vaskar	Vave
17	Vavekar	Vave
18	Verulkar	Verul
19	Virjolikar	Virjoli

W		
Sr. No.	**Surname**	**Village**
1	Wadavkar	Wadav
2	Wadhavkar	Wadhav
3	Wahatkar	Wahat
4	Wahralkar	Wahral
5	Wakrulkar	Wakrul
6	Wakarulkar	Wakrul
7	Walvatkar	Walvat
8	Walekar	Wali
9	Walwatkar	Walvati
10	Walvatkar	Walvati
11	Walvatnekar	Walvatne
12	Wandekar	Wande
13	Wandrekar	Wandre
14	Wargharkar	Warghari
15	Warulkar	Warul
16	Warvatnekar	Warvatne
17	Warshakar	Warshe
18	Warulkar	Warul
19	Warukar	Waru

20	Waskar	Waske
21	Watkar	Watke
22	Wavekar	Wave
23	Worlikar	Worli

X
None that I could find

Y		
Sr. No.	**Surname**	**Village**
1	Yawalkar	Yawal
2	Yeralkar	Yeral
3	Yerulkar	Yerul
4	Yulekar	Yule

Z		
Sr. No.	**Surname**	**Village**
1	Zarapkar	Zarap
2	Zarhapurkar	Zarhapur
3	Zharapkar	Zharap
4	Zavlikar	Zavli
5	Zawlikar	Zawli

An interesting point to note is that the Bene Israels being cautious as usual and in order to divest themselves of any peculiarities in the eyes of the locals, they Indianised their Hebrew names, for example Ezekiel became Hassaji, Benjamin Bunnaji, Abraham Abbaji and so on.

Many Bene Israels subsequently changed their surnames. Many adopted father's or the grandfather's name as their surnames or abridged their surnames, eg Ashtamkar to Ashton, Mhashilkar or Massilkar and it's other variationsto Massil and so on.

It is interesting to note that two surnames Alibaghkar and Revdankar were not very common amongst them.it is believed that these two towns were established much later when most Bene Israels had already adopted their surname, hence very few families took those names. However, it was still puzzling me, until I heard that there is a very interesting anecdote about how the town came to be known as Alibagh.

According to legend, there was a very rich Bene Israel merchant named Eli, who owned the complete area now known as Alibagh. It was inland of the Kulaba Fort. It was his wada (farm), also called as Bagh. People referred to it as Eli –Cha –Wada or Eli Cha Bagh i.e. Eli's farm, which people simplified and called it Elibagh .This name over a period of time, maybe several years or even a century or two, who knows, the Eli got mispronounced as Ali. Slowly the wada acquired the pseudonym Alibagh. Probably by then Eli was no more and his successors, who also over a period of years did not bother about it i.e. the change of name. Original land records were also not traceable. In recent years some politician wanted to change the name, but the locals objected to it. Frankly, I think it is time the authorities were made aware of it.

The Bene Israels were great pranksters and loved to pull each other's legs. A very common prank they played on each other was to attach some funny idiom or saying to an individual's surname. This was done either injest or in anger, I am not sure. Somehow these idioms stayed attached to those surnames, especially in the old days. I have managed to collect about 72 such idioms, which I have been collecting, again, since my childhood, just like the surnames, from grandmothers, aunts, uncles or any person who said them, I would immediately write them down. Hence, today I have this collection. Just like in the case of the surnames, these idioms are written against the surnames that are in alphabetical order. The idioms are then written in Marathi and the corresponding meaning in English, if I could decipher it or find out. If not, I have left a blank.

A		
1)	Agarwarkar	Aag Lavnara,	One who creates trouble for others.
2)	Alibaghkar	Mothi Pugdiwalla	Very egoistic.
3)	Ambepurkar	Karz Karnara	Always in debt.
4)	Astivkar	Ultya Khopdicha	Always irritated.
5)	Avedkar	Shanivar Sodnara	Always break the Shabbath.
6)	Awaskar	Dighe Mastewalla	---
B		
7)	Bamnolkar	Bombil Viknara	Selling Bombay ducks. (A type of fish.)
8)	Belkar	Veldore Khanara	Eats a lot of Cardamoms.
9)	Bhastekar	Por Viknara	Selling children.
10)	Bhonkar	Bhazun Khanara	Troubling people.
11)	Bhorankar	Phatke Zode Phatke	Torn shoes clumsy chalne walk.
12)	Borgavkar	Akshar Shunya	Uneducated.
C		
13)	Chincholkar	Bayaka Marnara	Beating Wives.
14)	Chordekar	Fukat Khanara	Eats free.
D		
15)	Dandoolkar	Wayit Budhiwall	Always thinks in the wrong sense.
16)	Dighorkar	Jawayche Aiknara	Listens to his son-in-law.
17)	Dhokarkar	Orduun Marnara	Yellsand beats.
18)	Divekar	Pumaaz Karnara	---
19)	Dodhkar	Karz Bazari	Always in debt.

F			
20)	Finjekar	Baikanna viknara	Selling wives.
G			
21)	Gadkar	Karkar Fuktachi Karkar	Grumble about nothing in particular.
22)	Galsurkar	Lokanche Paise	Cheat people Khanara of their money.
23)	Ghosalkar	Chindya Chandhya	Dresses in rags.
I			
23)	Ivlekar	Wede Pesse	Crazy
K			
24)	Kandlekar	Lach Khanare	Corrupt
25)	Kasukar	Garib Bechare	Poor thinking
26)	Kehimkar	Seva Karnara	Helpful
27)	Khanavkar	Radke Tond Karnara	Cranky face
28)	Kharilkar	Baikocha Bael	Bullied by wife.
29)	Khulabkar	Gondhal Ghalnara	Creates confusion.
30)	Killekar	Bata Karnara	Makes up stories.
31)	Kokbankar	Lavnya Ganara	Sings lavnis.
32)	Korlekar	Hundya Phodnara	Always angry,
33)	Kolatkar	Done Done Baika nakavar chasma	Having two wives with a big ego.
34)	Kurulkar	Kurkur Karnara	Grumble all the time.
M			
35)	Malekar	Ghar Jawai	Keeps son-in-law in the house

36)	Mazgaonkar	Mitkya Marnara	Always winking
37)	Mhashilkar	Maska Marnara	Sweet talker.
38)	Mhedekar	Baikanche Hukumat	Listens to wife's diktat. Manara
39)	Mordrekar	Kashyawari Tore	---
40)	Mheters	Gavat Nastil Tar	Create fights In the village.
	N		
41)	Nagavkar	Aatya Khanara	Always wrinkling forehead
42)	Nagotnekar	Narol Khanara	Eating coconut.
43)	Nawgharkar	Suki Mijash	Egoist
44)	Nawgavkar	Urkute	---
	P		
45)	Palkar	Namak Haram	Cannot be trusted.
46)	Penkar	Padnara	Releases gas.
47)	Pezarkar	Jawaicha Aiknara	Listens to son-in-law.
48)	Pingle	Konthud Phodnara	----
49)	Pugavkar	Fukte Khanara	Never pays for anything.
	R		
50)	Ramrazkar	Dalve Bael	---
51)	Razpurkar	Khandyavar Batwa	Show Off
52)	Revdandekar	Kavde Khanara	---
53)	Rohekar	Namaz Put Pir Buznar	---
	S		
55)	Saigavkar	Bokad Dandi	----
56)	Sankar	Daru Wiknara	Sells liquor

57)	Shapurkar	Ghus Khanara	Takes bribes and goes Turungat zanara to prison.
58)	Shapurkar	Khuni	Murderer
59)	Shirkolkar	Dadagiri Karnara	Bully
60)	Shirgavkar	Vare Sawre	Releases gas a lot.
61)	Shrivardhan	Shivya Denara	Abusive
T			
62)	Talkar	Ulti Khopdi	Crazy and lying Khote bolnara
63)	Tarankhopkar	Porila Avivahit	Keeping daughters Thevne unmarried.
64)	Thulkar	Kl Lavnara	Create fights and Tandul chornarasteals rice.
U			
65)	Umerdekar	Toplith Bharnara	Filling one's coffers.
V			
66)	Varulkar	Paise Zamavnara	Stingy
67)	Varvanjekar	Suka Khanara	Stingy
68)	Varkhanjenekar	Suka Khanara	Stingy
W			
69)	Wadavkar	Chikoo Marwadi	Very stingy
70)	Walvatkar	Val Khanara	Eats a lot of val.
71)	Wargharkar	Var Var Bolnara	Superficial talker.
72)	Waskar	Done Done Baikah	Having two wives.
73)	Waskar	Shanivar Todnara	Does not observe Shabbath.
Y			
74)	Yerulkar	Mathe Phiru	Strong headed

❏ ❏ ❏

CHAPTER
4

Various Professions of the Bene Israel's

The navy of the Marathas in the coastal region was being managed amd controlled by the Angrais whowere known as Kulabkar Angrais, because the fortress Kulaba became their headquarters, which was located on a promontory off the coastline of Alibagh. The surname Khulabkar and Kolabkar became the surnames of the Bene Israels from this place, the original name of which was Kulaba. Later on the area adjacent to the fortress was called Alibagh and the surrounding area as Kulaba district, which later became Kolaba district and further on,Colaba district.

As the Bene Israels got educated, they worked for the Marathas and the Angrais. They were hard working, honest, loyal and very good at their work, so they were rewarded in various ways. They were given a lot of privileges in the form of land allotments,wadas, exemption of taxes etc. The privileges were constituted on legal documents called 'Sanad'. Many families were honored with these privileges. According to the Ashtamkar Sanad, special honors were granted to all the members of the oil pressing community. They were exempt from house tax, they could exercise the rights of Mheters i.e. village officers, that too from one generation to the next.

From the three Kajis appointed by David Rahabi, the three families were conferred with hereditary rights to be called as Kajis and act as officiating priests with the approval of the Angrais. Though their headquarters were mainly in Alibagh, Revdanda, Ambepur, Parud and Murud, they travelled wherever their services were required and even settled community disputes with the help of influential men within the community wherever there was a dispute. For their services they received fees, as well as travelling and other expenses.

A Royal edict issued in 1761, is the first known written reference to the Kajis, wherein it is mentioned that a Bene Israel Kaji in the Bene Israel hierarchy has to be given his due honors and respect, to which he is entitled.

Thus, they were given special honors and were accorded precedence in every ceremony and festivity. They were entitled to a double share in the feast after birth, marriage, death, fulfillment of a vow etc. The Kajis were exempted from house tax and cattle tax and were entitled to procure gratuitous labor whenever they required it.

Under the British Government, the Bene Israel Kajis in Bombay were employed in succession on a monthly salary to administer the oath to the Bene Israels in court. Now for the last 30,40 or more years, these appointments have been dispensed with.

Furthermore, as the Kajis had not kept up with the times, there was a gradual waning of the respect shown to them. When the synagogues were built, they i.e. the Kajis, organized the community into a sort of a congregation under the leadership of a Mukkadam (leader), assisted by 4 or 5 elderly counselors from within the community called Choglas. They also appointed a Gabbai (treasurer), then a Hazan (reader) who was either a Cochini, a Bagdadi or a Yeminite Jew and who also performed the duties of a Shohet (slaughterer), Mohel (one who performs circumcisions) and

Sopher (teacher), a Shamash (caretaker) who also functioned as a source of information about the community members. The Jamat (i.e. the congregation) consisted of all its male members. There was no Rabbi and till 2015, there is still no Rabbi. The Kajis also helped in organizing the administration for new Bene Israel Synagogues.

According to the Sanad of 1840, confirming the Sanad of 1770, in turn confirming the hereditary rights to the Kajis, which stipulated legally, they enjoy inheritance of these rights and privileges as Kajis. This was specifically conferred on Yacob Elloji and his brothers. They could conduct marriages, funeral services, circumcision ceremonies and settle caste disputes. They were also granted the right to enjoy all the previous privileges as before, and any labor that they would employ would be gratuitous.

A Sanad was also granted by the Peshwa Government to Abraham Kaji and Dawud Kaji of Rajapuri.

The Ashtamkars have a Sanad referring to the land they owned by them in Ashtami for generations. One Aaron Charikar was appointed Naik or Commander of a fleet by Kanoji Angrai at the beginning of the 17th century. He also received a Sanad of being granted hereditary privileges and land holdings.

Some Prominent Bene Israel's of those Times

In Kihim, lived a man Aaron who had 4 sons, Elloji, Abaji, Bhawji and Essaji. After their father's death, they moved to Nadgam. Elloji had a son Joseph, who went to live in Ramraj after his father's death. Jacob was his son, who had large land holdings, cattle, rice fields and a wada in Ramraj. He was also a money lender. His house was plundered and burnt many times. Ultimately he was reduced to poverty. His grandson Shalom Samuel Kehimkar is still in possession of some of his land. Annually this land yields income from the procurement of rice.

Another Bene Israel, Bapuji Doodhkar lived during the reign of the Angrais. He traded in oil from Jafrabad, tobacco from Ghats and Surat, betelnut from Konkan, sandalwood from the Malabar, cotton from Coomta, as well as spices and other commodities. He had his own ships, wherewith he traded with other ports. He managed his business well, and amassed considerable wealth, but only for some time. All his ware houses were burnt in a great fire.

Several Bene Israel families were also conferred with the title of Naik.

Bene Israel's even today are gallant and faithful soldiers, as they have proved themselves time and again. It is a well-known fact that bravery, courage, nobility and majesty of features are characteristics of the Hebrew race all over the world, in spite of differences in dress and local customs. Israelites have inherited soldier like qualities because of the royal race from where they have descended. Hence, they are ill accustomed to slavery and their look shows recollection of and consciousness of great destinies. Courage has been the most distinctive feature of the Hebrew race, to which their survival is attributed and which may be associated with the fact that Israelites have been motivated by the proverb

"Nobility imposes great obligations and responsibilities."

Recollections of the heroic deeds of their ancestors, the memories of their undaunted valor on the battlefields and many other qualities have produced many gallant soldiers amongst the Bene Israels, who have rushed into battle under furious charges of musketry and have also faced canons. They have proved themselves by their faithfulness, firmness of resolutions and other mental qualities, to be the descendants of a mighty race of warriors. They are those who have defeated the most powerful armies, under terribly trying circumstances in the holy land.

Bene Israels were found in the armies in England, France, Spain, Germany, Italy, Turkey, Austria, Prussia, Russia, India and many others countries during various wars.

The earliest mention of Bene Israel soldiers is the case of 2 members of the Charikar family, who were appointed as Commodores of the navy by the Abyssinion rulers of Janjira, who had to fight with soldiers of the Angrais. In this battle the Angrais captured them. The Angrais then asked them to join their ranks. When they refused to turn traitors, they were massacred in cold blood. Being convinced of their loyalty and bravery, the Angrais appointed 2 Bene Israels from the Charikar family itself, one Samuel (Samaji) and the other

Abraham (Alloji) to command their navy. As a token for their faithful service, the government of the Angrais granted the Charikar family land as Inam (gift) which is still with the family. Also special honors were reserved for the community.

Several other Bene Israels rose to eminence at the time of the Peshwas and Angrais. Several families such as the Waskars and Malekars received Inams. The ancestors of the Gadkar family were nominated as Commandants of Sagadgad Fort in Alibagh. The family got their surname Gadkar because of that, otherwise they were known as Wadhavkars. Similarly, the Bhorapkars who were in charge of the Bhorap fort and many others such as the Ashtamkars, Shirgavkars, Nagawkars, Thulkars, Warvatnekars etc, many of whom were later appointed as Mheters i.e. Village Officers.

Many Bene Israels did not rise to great positions and affluence because according to them, their religion did not permit them to assimilate with the natives, nor was there anybody to speak on their behalf, is what they believed.

Many joined the armies of Shivaji and served in various posts, not only as fighters, but also on the administrative side, such as store keeping, stock taking, looking after Shivaji's forts, accounts and many other areas. They did extremely well in whichever job they undertook. They were sincere and hardworking and hence prospered. Many Bene Israel families were rewarded with land and wadas. Many of their descendents still enjoy it, while some others, due to their habits were reduced to penury.

Until the reign of Raghoji Angria (1790 – 1838), none of the local rulers showed any interest in the Bene Israels. Raghoji Angrai and one of his ministers Vinayak Parshuram Bivalkar, instituted an inquiry into the religions of the Mohamedans and the Bene Israels. Their curiosity was aroused when the Bene Israels as usual, had gone to bless Raghoji Angrai and his minister, the morning after Yom Kippur. On being questioned and asked to give their details, Samuel Jacob Kehimkar, gave a detailed account of the Jewish race right from the time of creation, the names of some important descendents and incidents of their history.

Raghoji Angrai and his minister were surprised to learn that the lineage of the Shanivar Tellis was so interesting and that it established a continuous link from creation to the latest times. They were so impressed that they wanted to give him an award. Since S. J. Kehimkar was employed by the British, the only gift that they could give him was to exempt him from house tax, for his house was in Alibagh, till such time as his house was in his possession.

❑ ❑ ❑

Sojourn in Bombay

The Bene Israels were skeptical and initially did not come to Bombay. They felt that since the island is open on all sides, attacks by foreign troops were always a possibility. Then again, the island was a very unhealthy place. It was always pervaded by an offensive odor. Also, it was a place infested with pestilence and many people would become victims of various diseases like Cholera, Influenza, Small Pox, Plague etc. The Bene Israels hesitated to move until they were sure of the policies of the British with regard to their governance and their religious tolerance, which was most important to them.

When the island of Bombay came into the possession of the East India Company, many Bene Israels came to Bombay, expecting more religious freedom. They did not come earlier while it was in the hands of the Portuguese, being afraid lest they might have the same fate as many of those Indian races including the Jews, who were forced to embrace Christianity against their will or face torture. This happened to the Portuguese Jews in Goa.

Garcia de Orta, a Portuguese Jew and a renowned physician had arrived in Goa in 1534 and settled there. In 1534, the Portuguese had obtained the islands of Bombay together with Bassein and the island of Salsette, through a treaty with the Sultan of Gujarat, Bahadur Shah Zafar. In 1548 the Portuguese Viceroy gave Garcia one island on annual rent, which is today the city of Mumbai. The island was then called Mombayin or Bom Bayia, which means 'good bay' and constituted Malabar Hill and Girgaum. This island was rented out to Garcia de Orta in recognition of his services rendered to the Portuguese in Goa as he was a physician of great repute and was also called by the Indian Royals for his services.

He was a devout practicing Jew. He observed the Shabbath, Yom Kippur and all the festivals. He strictly observed the Mosaic laws. He died in Goa and was buried in his house on the quiet, as the Portuguese did not know that he was a devout Jew, they thought he was a Christian.

It was during the inquisition, when Garcia's sister Catharina and her husband were caught and under duress gave a full account of how her brother's funeral was performed as per the Jewish tradition. In 1569, Catharina and her husband were tied to the pillars and burnt in their synagogue in Goa, which was part of their house and which today is probably a church. And according to some, the same church where the body of St Francis Xavier is kept. When the Portuguese learnt of this, they exhumed Garcia's body, burnt it and threw his ashes into the sea, as a form of punishment. Interestingly, it was the Portuguese themselves, who, while they were in India, issued a postage stamp in his honor. Ironic, but true.

His earlier biographers referred to him as a devout Christian. In 1934, Dr. Walter Pischel brought out the true picture that Garcia was secretly practicing Judaism, which he could not do openly because of the religious intolerance of the Portuguese.

When the island of Bombay came into the hands of the East India Company, the British government adopted the policy of religious tolerance and freedom.

Once their apprehensions cleared, many Bene Israels moved to Bombay. They enlisted in the British army and did well.

In Bombay, many Bene Israels entered the company services and secured all the posts in the military service that were open to them because of their bravery, loyalty and faithfulness. As mentioned earlier, many Bene Israels gained distinction in military service.

Mention must be made of one Subedar Daniel Khurrilkar whose distinguished service was formulated in the form of a letter and he was awarded an unusually large sized gold medal. This medal is still in the possession of the subsequent generations of his family.

However, not with standing the distinguished services rendered by the Bene Israels, the high officials of the government never inquired as to who these people were, what role they played in the history of this country, nor whether they were rewarded or honored in recognition of their distinguished services with appointments as Native Aid–De–Camps on the personnel staff of His Excellency, the Governor or Commander–In–Chief.

The claim that the Bene Israels were always ignored was brought out in a report by His Excellency Lord Harris, the late Governor of Bombay who showed interest in the community. In the course of his speech, at the prize distribution ceremony of the Israelite school in 1893, he said and I quote a few excerpts, "that the Bene Israel community supplied gallant and loyal soldiers to the British army in India, but they were not mentioned in their reports. That the community will continue to supply recruits to the Native Army and that because of their own efforts, there are men who are rising to distinguished positions in that profession. Subsequently they rose to the rank of Native Officers. In the British army, the highest rank for native officers was Subedar, Subedar Commandant and Subedar Major."

Thus, with the coming of the British, many Bene Israels moved to Bombay (now Mumbai) and joined the British army, again excelling in various jobs within the army service. They were further posted to Poona (Pune), Ahmedabad and other places such as Gujarat, Karachi, Burma, in fact all over the subcontinent, where again they prospered and also built synagogues.

They also joined the Navies of the Siddis, who are Muslims of Abyssinian origin, who had conquered parts of the Konkan. The

Angrais were the powerful Maratha naval commanders, who ruled the Konkan coast till the Europeans gained superiority in the region. The Siddis never lost Jangira and it was merged with the Indian Union in 1948. As within the armies and the navies of Shivaji, in the British armies and navies also, the Bene Israels distinguished themselves. Their names can be found in the Roll of Honor in the various forts they worked in and also in the Roll of Honor of The Maratha Light Infantry, Grenadiers and Bombay Sappers and various other regiments.

Prominent among them is Samuel Ezekiel Divekar (Samaji Hasaji Divekar) who was the native commandant (Subedar Major) in the Bombay Presidency Army. During the Mysore wars, he was captured along with the other native Officers and men by Tipu Sultan. He escaped the death sentence on the intervention of Tipu's mother who heard that he was a Bene Israel and told her son that these people were mentioned in the Quran with favor. After retirement, Samuel Ezekiel Divekar built the "Shaar Ha Rahamim" synagogue in Bombay in 1796, as he had promised himself, that if he got out alive he would build a synagogue for the community. It was the first synagogue to be built in India. The street where the synagogue was built is named in his honor "Samuel Street".

The medals of Samuel Issaji, who was a part of the Third Regiment of the Bombay native Infantry 1824 – 1871, are still preserved at the Maratha Regimental centre at Belgaum. He was honored with the title of Sardar Bahadur, Honorary Captain and was decorated with the Order of British India.

Abraham Samuel was a Havaldar Major of 102 Infantry in 1878 and subsequently was with the Grenadiers. There were many Bene Israel Subedar Majors and Havaldar Majors who did yeoman service for the country during the British rule.

Another story of assimilation of the Bene Israels and their rise to prominence, showing a unique example of a Jew and Muslim sharing power, is the story of the Wargharkar family. Jacob B Israel got land in Warghari village as a reward for his services to the Angrais. Hence he and his family were called Wargharkars. Later they adopted the surname Israel.

Abrahamji Wargharkar was enlisted in the Fourth Rifles Regiment of the English Bombay Presidency Army and soon became a Havaldar Major, a high rank for a native soldier. He was sent on a military expedition to China which preceded the first Opium War of 1839. He never returned from that expedition. His brother Soloman (Silleman / Satkelji) was also a Havaldar in the 25thregiment of the Bombay Native Light Infantry.

Abrahamji's son, Ezekiel (Bapuji) was enlisted as a boy recruit into his father's regiment, as he had become an orphan after the death of his father and his mother had died in his childhood. He joined as a sepoy, worked hard and soon became a Subedar in 22 years of service and then sought retirement. He received two medals, Mooltan and Persia. He could not attain the highest rank Subedar Major, as he had lost all his teeth and was not able to give the drill commands as effectively as was required. He then joined the police force and settled down in Ahmednagar for the education of his sons, Shalom and Jacob Wargharkars, who later in life became Karbharis (Prime Ministers) of two princely states.

Shalom Bapuji became the karbhari of the state of Janjira under the Nawab Sidi Ahmed Khan. Jacob Bapuji became karbhari of the state of Aundh. After retirement he immersed himself in community work. Shalom Bapuji's son Hyam Shalom was a graduate and was a karbhari of the State of Akalkot in 1917 during the reign of Raja Saheb F. S. Bhosale.

Benjamin J Israel (Wargharkar) born inAugust 1906 and died January in 1987 is remembered for his pioneering scholarly research concerning the Bene Israel community. He mentions in his book 'Jews of India', about a medical officer Captain Aaron Joseph MBBS, son of Dr Joseph Benjamin of Ahmedabad. In World War I, he served as a medical officer under the British General Edmund Allenby, in Mesopotamia, Egypt and Palestine. He entered Jerusalem with General Allenby in 1917. Later he was bombed and shell shocked in the fighting at Kantara and returned back as the army returned. He died in 1924.

❑ ❑ ❑

Customs they Adopted
from their Neighbors

The ancestors of the Bene Israels adopted certain peculiar customs regarding puberty, pregnancy, child birth, marriages etc. from the other local communities such as the Hindus and the Muslims. Most of these customs and ceremonies have been discontinued because of religious enlightenment which made them aware that the customs they were observing in their ignorance were not in accordance with Mosaic laws. Although in some families it is so ingrained, that they still observe them.

Early marriages were common amongst the Bene Israels. Children 8 or 10 years old were married, a custom familiar since Biblical times, though as per the Talmud, it has been laid down that unless a boy is 13 and a day old and a girl 12 and a day old, they should not marry.

Out of all the peculiar customs prevalent, I would like to mention a few regarding marriages which were an imitation of the local customs.

Fixing of an auspicious day for the marriage, calling of 5 individuals or unmarried women for every occasion, putting on green bangles on the wrist of the bride a day before the wedding, waving of copper or silver coins around the bride and groom to avert the evil spirits, throwing rice on the couple as a sign of fertility, putting mehendi on their hands and feet on the previous day, fastening together the hems of their handkerchief as a symbol of their union, tying of a necklace called a lacha made of glass and golden beads around the neck of the bride at the conclusion of the marriage ceremony; making the newly-weds pull out rolls of leaves or cloves held between their teeth from the mouths of each other, making them play various such intimate games. Also Bene Israeli husband and wife, copying Hindu customs, did not address each other by their personal names. Amongst many Bene Israel families even today, at the end of the marriage ceremony, the bridegroom ties a lacha around the bride's neck, difference being that instead of glass beads, it is a gold chain with interwoven black beads, just like the Hindus.

Another peculiar custom was the breaking of the bangles and the lacha worn by the woman after the death of her husband and she had to discontinue wearing any ornaments including the nose ring and only dress in white. Fortunately, this custom is totally abolished since a really long time, exactly how long I do not know. I have not seen it performed in my lifetime. Unfortunately, there was no such dress code prescribed for the gents after the death of their wives.

Our ancestors introduced these local customs, probably because at that point in time, circumstances must have compelled them to practice it. Most of these customs have been discontinued but many families still practice these customs and rituals as if they are a part of Jewish observances. Unfortunately, this ignorance continues even today.

The mehendi ceremony today is observed with a lot of pomp and ceremony, involving a lot of expenditure. They have become theme occasions. Also the original lacha is now compulsorily made of black beads with interwoven gold patterns and the bride has to wear green bangles, just like the Hindus. People claim that it is done for the fun it involves, but what I have seen and the way it is done conveys a different picture.

Today, though marriages are solemnized when both the boy and the girl are adults, the parents or guardians still take the lead in making a choice of a partner, with the consent of the youngsters. Many families introduce the youngsters and let them decide if they would like to take the relationship further. Love marriages are also common, both with one partner being from within the community or outside the community. Mixed marriages are rampant.

Mention must also be made about the slaughtering of a chicken, immediately after a circumcision and when the chicken is cooked it is served only to the guests. The immediate family members do not eat it; the reason I feel is because it is sacrificial. Also, one does not want to waste good chicken meat, so it is served to the guests. The funny part is that the guests are given one piece per person as if it is Prasad (amongst the Hindus after their pujas, they give a small quantity of something sweet to every attendee as a sign of ??).

There are some customs and practices followed by a few, but their numbers are insignificant. I must mention a peculiar custom following the birth of a child, which I witnessed. For forty days after delivery, the woman and the child are placed in a room with very few clothes on and in the corner of the room, a coal fire is lit. For some time the new mother is asked to sit on a chair which has crossed trellis work and which is placed over the fire, so the heat of the fire reaches her private parts. There is a lot of smoke created in the room. The new mother and the new born baby have to inhale that smoke. I was shocked to see it. I tried to explain to the family that this was very unhealthy. They are both inhaling a lot of carbon dioxide, which is not good for either of them. It will affect their breathing. Fortunately that family saw reason and promised to discontinue the practice. I told them to spread the correct message. Surprisingly, what I had witnessed was in Mumbai and not in the villages. There, the people are more enlightened.

❑ ❑ ❑

CHAPTER
8

Various Committees
and Institutions

The Jews of Bombay were very enterprising and had several members in various committees. These committees had to over see the work of the community. There was the Bene Israel Nirasrith Fund; one aspect of its job was to oversee the functioning of an old age home they had established. The old age home was in the same building, which housed the Stree Mandal, behind the Magen Hassidim synagogue, in Nagpada. A Bene Israel philanthropist donated the entire building and various floors were utilized for different activities. On the ground floor was the Stree Mandal, if I remember right, then there was a floor where young women were taught sewing, embroidery, darning, knitting etc.

On one of the floors was the old age home. I was most fascinated by it. I have visited it often with my mother Dr. Grace Moses, an MBBS DGO, who used to visit the old age home once a week on Thursdays which used to be a holiday for schools in those days. She took me there some times. There was another physician, a male doctor Dr. Samuel, an M.D. i.e. a medical specialist, who visited the home also once a week but on another day.

I don't remember the drawing room but I clearly remember the dining room and the bedrooms of the inmates. The dining room had a huge ornate teak table where about 20 people could sit. There were 20 chairs around it also made of teak. Each inmate had his/her room, or also shared a room, with a palang (Huge ornate high bed) so that the old people had no problem getting on or off the bed. Each inmate also had a cupboard where they kept their belongings. Everything was always very neat and clean. All the furniture was made of teak, donated by various Bene Israels with their names engraved on metal plates and fixed on the respective furniture piece and also made by Bene Israel carpenters who were the best. The furniture was really something, excellent.

There was a female and a male caregiver to look after the inmates and cater to their needs, if required even bathe and dress them. Also there was a Bene Israel cook who cooked kosher meals for the inmates including any specific diet the inmates had to follow. Once or twice a week they were given meat and once or twice a week fish. On festival days, one of the trust board members, may be with his family would say the prayers there with the inmates. The inmates had a choice whether they wanted to contribute something towards their upkeep or nothing at all. Some did, most didn't. Besides, there was no fixed amount that they had to give. Some well-to-do inmates had their own bank accounts which they operated or asked some staff member to operate it for them. The home was run mainly on voluntary donations. There were no thefts or any pilferage.

I remember one inmate, a tall, very fair well-to-do lady, fairly well educated. She had a lot of her own money and jewelry. She always donated a lot of money towards the old age home. I remember her jewelry because she had a lot of it and because she has shown it to me on several occasions while my mother made her rounds. My mother had told her that I wanted to become a doctor, so she would always encourage me to study a lot. She wanted me to take her jewelry but my mother and I always said no it is yours. She was alone in this world as her husband was dead and she had no children.

I also remember an elderly male in his 70s who was severely diabetic and was bedridden. But the care he got was so good that he did not have any bedsores and was always jovial to talk to.

Later, both the caregivers got old themselves, one wanted to go to Israel with his family, while the other felt just too old and tired. The trustees had three lawyers on their committee, one of whom was my father Ephraim Moses, Advocate High Court. One of the by-laws of the old age home was that they could not employ a couple as caregivers. They advertised a lot but somehow could not get anyone. There was a couple that had come from Israel who were desperate to get the job. The committee members were split, the lawyers against it. While voting, those for the couple won and they were installed there. That was the downfall of the old age home.

One philanthropist donated his bungalow in the hill station of Matheran, to the Bene israels. It is a huge place with a lot of land surrounding it. I had been there as a child. It is in a pretty isolated area scary especially at night. Today, it is not so scary as the local population has increased, as has also the number of tourists.

The Bene Israels also had a Jewish sanatorium in Panchgani, a hill station near Pune, where the climate was always cool (unlike today) and the air was clean and fresh and where all those suffering from tuberculosis were looked after and brought back to health.

There was an educational trust that ran purely on donations and helped the poor students of the community. The Bene Israel Benevolent Society to help the needy Bene Israels was founded in 1853 by Haeem Samuel Kehimkar. It was functioning till of late.

CHAPTER
9

Population and Common Residential Areas

The population of the Bene Israels at any given point in time was never too many. Still it may be reasonable to assume that over several years, the Bene Israel population could have been sizable, though the exact numbers are not known and which slowly dwindled with the mass migration when it slipped to about 30,000, which has been documented but the exact years are not known. Then, in 1951 according to the census, it fell to 20,000 and by 1960 it further fell to 12,000. According to the 1991 census of India, the numbers further dwindled to a total of 5271 with 2766 males and 2505 females. At present, there are about 5000 Jews in India.

An article in the Times of India, Pune edition, dated Wednesday, July 2nd 2003, titled "Jews struggle to keep their faith".

Excerpts – "There is a definite decline in religious observances in recent years. Today people identify themselves as Jewish merely because they were born in the Jewish community, not because they actually follow the religion. Today's youngsters are more concerned about their careers, inter-caste marriages are widespread and the atmosphere cosmopolitan."

Old Jewish mohallas as they were called in the old days, for instance, in Mumbai, the areas were Dongri, Sandhurst Road, Mazagaon, J J Hospital area, Byculla, Jacob Circle and many others. There were also Jewish mohallas in Pune, Ahmedabad, Konkan areas and many other places, which today have practically vanished. This is not only because of the migration out of the country, but also the scattering of the community, moving to less crowded, healthier areas and hence moving out of the main city /town towards the outskirts. Still, in some places especially in the Konkan, they are still referred to as Jewish mohallas. These mohallas were usually in and around the synagogues where Jews lived and attended services in the synagogues. Either the synagogue was built where the Jews lived or the Jews lived wherever there was a Jewish synagogue, thus making it convenient to attend services.

The mass exodus left behind only few Bene Israels, barely a few hundreds in some cities, tens in the others and much less in the villages of the Konkan. The numbers are slightly more in bigger cities like Mumbai, which has the maximum number; Pune has about 250, less in Ahmedabad, Delhi and other places in India. As per the last census, today i.e. in 2015, the community totals only about 5000 in the whole of India.

The beauty of all this is that, especially in the Konkan area as one walks through the roads, lanes and by lanes, you can still see the mezuzah on the door post, even in the homes of the Muslims who bought the houses from the Jews. When asked, they said that if this protects your homes, it will also protect our homes too and we will never remove it. What was more surprising is that both Hindus and Muslims kiss the mezuzah as they enter or leave their homes. Also, I observed that in many homes, the brass mezuzahs were shining, which means that the owners regularly polish them. The Bene Israels have left them this beautiful legacy.

The decline in the population has affected the attendance in the synagogues. Even on Sabbath, it is difficult to get a minyan (a quorum of 10 men required for Torah reading and reading of certain other prayers). However, during major festivals and at weddings, the synagogues still have a good attendance.

❑ ❑ ❑

Education and
Musical Talent

From 296 BC to 1000 AD, there was lack of education amongst the Bene Israels. They were sunk in total ignorance. Their ancestors, having come from the northern part of Palestine i.e. Galilee, the knowledge that they brought from there must have been very little, because Galilee in those days did not offer the educational advantage which the province of Judea provided with Jerusalem as its centre.

In Galilee, because of their close proximity with the Syrians and Samarians, their minds were contaminated with heathen beliefs and superstitions, belief in evil spirits, demonical possessions and miraculous cures. But what it lacked in higher education, it made up in morality. The Talmud comments on the moral superiority of the Jews of Galilee over the Judeans.

The initial impact on the Bene Israel Jewish observances and on the religious musical compositions, were derived mainly from the Cochini traditions, which were themselves a fusion of Sephardic,

Yemenite, Babylonian and other influences. Yemenite Hazanim officiated at the prayers services for the Bene Israels stationed in Aden, where the British in civil and military posts employed them since 1839. In course of time, Yemenite cantors and their families officiated at the Bene Israel synagogues and prayer halls in India. Also Hazzanim from the Baghdadi community of Bombay officiated at the prayers services at the Bene Israel synagogues. Recently, a few European Jewish melodies (Ashkenazi) have become a part of the Bene Israel tunes.

During the British Raj, in the 1930's and 1940's, there was an upsurge of musical talent in the form of prayers, chants and hymns in Hebrew and Marathi. They also wrote lyrics specific to Jewish life in both Hebrew and Marathi. There is a large compilation of songs in Marathi, which they wrote on themes from the psalms and Biblical figures. There were two well known musicians who were very good mandolin players, Isaac David Dandekar and Faizulla Tagloff.

A youth group was formed in Bombay in 1935 called Habonim. They introduced a number of patriotic songs about Palestine, later Israel and also songs in the Ashkenazi tradition. Simeon Jacob Kharilkar was a good singer in the community in the old days.

Gauhar Jan, who was born in 1873 and whose parents were Armenian Jews, was the first to record a song in Calcutta. She sat in front of a recording horn in a makeshift studio where some of the first recordings were made in India by her.

The pre-independence recordings of Jewish songs and music was released as a compilation by researchers who took 5 years collecting and compiling songs of the few Bene Israel musicians, such as Simeon Jacob Kharilkar, Nathan S Satamkar and Isaac Jacob David Dandekar.

A few Bene Israels also excelled in fine arts and creative writing.

From 1690 to 1740, there was one Bene Israel Elloji Nagawkar / Elloji Shahir i.e. Elloji, the Ballad singer. He enjoyed the patronage of the Angrai Rulers and performed in the Peshwa court. Some of his songs in Marathi and Hindi on religious and moral issues are remembered till today and became famous. He was born in 1690 and lived till 1740. He was a composer of Hindi and Marathi songs, especially Lavni. He used to be invited to the Peshwa Court in Poona. His songs were very popular and all the Bene Israels used to sing his songs. Unfortunately, as there were few printing presses, very few of his songs and poems exist today, probably with some of his family members. Historians often wondered how Biblical themes and Hebrew words were prevalent in his songs and how he was so conversant with these languages at such an early date in History.

Another famous Bene Israel singer Reubenji Isaji Nawgaonkar/ Reubenji Shahir was born in 1830. He was another ballad singer. He was a poet, a composer and a great dreamer. He was well versed in Marathi, English and Hebrew. He left his father's home and came to Bombay where he worked as a clerk for the British. But all he was focused on were songs, especially Lavnis, (folk poetry and dance), in which he was a prolific writer and which practically engulfed his life. Most of the time, he neglected his family because of his passion.

In the 19th century, Bene Israels introduced a form of song called Kirtan, the word actually means song in Marathi. It was a typically Hindu form used for religious education of the masses. The Bene Israel Kirtans were Bible stories, presented in Marathi verse, either sung solo or in chorus with or without instrumental accompaniment.

A kirtan about Queen Esther was written by one of the most prolific kirtan composers, Benjamin Samson Ashtamkar. It was performed on 6th January 1895.Another episode was performed during the Maccabees festival on 2nd February 1896. These were performed in the Share Rason Synagogue. Each performance was followed by a different lecture, which means two different lectures.

In those days, there were groups who sang these songs at nightlong sessions. Reubenji Shahir was heading one such group. He would often introduce Hebrew words and verses into his Lavnis. His granddaughter Rebecca Reuben subsequently became the principal of the Israelite school.

The missionary translation of the Bible into Marathi was the original inspiration for the Bene Israel kirtans. In the 1840s, Cochini teachers in collaboration with the Bene Israels published translations of Jewish prayers in Marathi. Also, they published a book of songs and a book of rules for fixing the dates of the various Jewish festivals. Thus the Bene Israel spirit surged and flowered in the 1850s.

In 1837 Rev Dr. Wilson's attention was directed towards the Bene Israels. He opened vernacular schools in Alibagh, Revdanda, Pen, Panvel, Nagaon, Ambepur, Ashtami and many other places with ulterior motives. He wanted to encourage Christian education amongst the children of the Bene Israels. Luckily, they had many Bene Israel teachers who stuck to their subjects and encouraged the children to know about Judaism.

Between 1810 and 1812, a lot of missionary schools sprang up in Bombay and the Konkan. Many Bene Israel children joined these schools. Hebrew was not one of the subjects. So Mr Haeem Jacob Kehimkar started a school where Hebrew was taught. As the student numbers increased, later and with great efforts, he started the Israelite school at Mazagaon.

Actually in 1875, Mr Haeem Jacob Kehimkar, Joseph Samuel Kehimkar and A. D. Pezarkar started a school that taught both Hebrew and Marathi. For this they were approached by some youngsters to open a Hebrew and Marathi school for the children of the community and they promised they would willingly contribute. But Mr Haeem Jacob Kehimkar knew his people well. He knew that they will be interested initially but will not show any interest later on. That they will keep on finding faults with some thing or the other. So at first he did not give the project much thought. However there were repeated appeals, so he finally met Shallom Samuel Kehimkar and they opened a school on 5th July, 1875. It was called the Hebrew – Marathi School.

Due to lack of funds, they requested the Anglo Jewish Association of London to help out. They responded generously and finally on 1st April 1881, the school came under their patronage and became known as the Israelite School. The committee kept telling all the

Bene Israels to take advantage of the school. Later, Government aid was sought which was granted at Rs 1560/- per annum. They increased it to Rs 2000/- annually.

David Sassoon and Co was also approached for their liberal aid to the school. They gave only Rs 400/- annually from 1st October 1882. On further requests, they increased it to Rs 600/- per year from 1st April 1888 to meet the increasing expenses. After the demise of Mr. S. D. Sassoon, they reverted to the original amount of Rs 400/- per annum from 1st April 1895. As expenses increased, further appeals were made to the community and the synagogue authorities. The premise being that if our people did not sympathize with the needs of the children of our own community, how could you expect others to sympathize with us. The Anglo Jewish Foundation of London also asked them to try and meet the increasing expenses from within their own community. Support was later granted by the Kadoori family on the condition that the name should be changed to 'The Sir Eli Kadoori School'.

Michael Sargon, a Cochini Jew who had converted to Christianity came to Bombay in 1826 and established 6 Hebrew Marathi schools in Bombay, Alibagh, Revdanda, Ashtami and Palli. He taught the Bene Israels everything about Judaism. Besides,he knew Hebrew, English and Marathi. He worked for their religious upliftment until his death in Surat on the 1st of June 1870 at the age of 80.

Subsequently in 1833, many Cochinis Jews came and rendered great service to the Bene Israels. Some translated the prayer books into Marathi with the help of the Bene Israels themselves.

Shellomo Salem Shurrabi in 1840, published the Selihoth in Marathi. Hyam Joseph Halegoa translated the Hebrew Passover service i.e. the Haggada into Marathi with the help of Hyeem Essaji Garsulkar in1845. Obadia Zackai in 1846 translated the Hebrew Shiroth (song book) into Marathi. In 1845, David Judah Ashkenazi translated the Hebrew Almanac that contains the rules for fixing days of observance for 500 years into Marathi.

Ezekiel Rahabi's letter of 1768, mentions that prior to 1768, sometimes the Bene Israels sought guidance from the Cochini leaders. He also mentions one Bene Israel who studied in Cochin for 4 years.

A group of dedicated Cochini Jewish teachers arrived in the Konkan in1826, followed by another group in 1833. They brought about a religious revival not only in Bombay, but also in Revdanda, Alibagh, Ashtami and Palli, where they worked as teachers, preachers and interpreters of the Bible and Jewish law.

Amongst the Jewish teachers from Cochin, Shelomo Salem Shurrabi was outstanding. In 1838, while coming from Cochin along with his grandfather, they were shipwrecked at Nawgaon. Shelomo's grandfather drowned, while Shelomo was rescued and nursed back to health by a Bene Israel man from Alibagh. Thereafter he devoted himself to teaching Judaism. He served as Hazan in the Shaare Rason synagogue consecrated in1844, till his death on a salary of Rs 100/- per annum. He also helped establish many other synagogues in Bombay, Revdanda(1846), Alibagh (1848) and Panvel (1849). He was also a Mohel, Shohet and a book-binder. He died in 1856.

Cochini Jews took the Bene Israels closer to mainstream Judaism. The Yemenite influences were because of the Bene Israels staying in Aden. Eventually, Yemenite Hazanim came to officiate in some of the Bene Israel synagogues and prayer halls even in the Konkan. The first Torah scrolls that the Bene Israels received came from Yemen via Aden.

Earlier, later and even today, though microscopic in numbers, the Bene Israels have given the country judges, advocates, doctors, engineers, architects, army, navy and air force officers, including so far 3 Generals and 1 Admiral, teachers, actors and many other professionals, you just name it. Many Bene Israels have excelled in their respective professions and made a name for themselves and brought laurels to India.

The late ex-Prime Minister of India Mrs. Indira Gandhi, in a speech which she delivered in 1968, as the chief guest in the Cochin

Pardeshi Synagogue at its 400th centenary celebration said and I quote "The Jewish community in India has rendered and continues to render valuable service in many fields. It has contributed distinction in business, industry, civil services, armed forces and others."

Three Bene Israels were awarded with the prestigious Padma Shree Award of India. They are:

1- Dr Jerusha Jhirad, who won it in 1966.

2- David Abraham Cheulkar, in 1969, and

3- Dr Reuben David Dandekar in 1975, an imaginative superintendent of the Ahmedabad zoo and founder of the Ahmedabad children's park.

The Bene Israel community was thriving and throbbing in the 1600's, 1700's 1800's and early part of the 1900's, when it gradually started dwindling. After Israel's independence in 1948, more migration took place not only from the cities but also from most of the Konkan villages. The migration was not only to Israel, but also to England, USA, Canada, Australia and elsewhere.

Mass migrations started to the Holy land, after Israel got its independence in 1948. During the early days, the Rabbis in Israel raised the question about whether the Bene Israels were really Jews, because of their long stay in India and their Indian ways. A recent study on the genetic material of the Bene Israels by a British scientist Dr. Tudor Parfitt, a professor of Jewish studies at London's School of Oriental and African Studies, has proved them to be direct descendants of the Cohanims, who are hereditary Israelite priests of the Second Temple of Jerusalem.

Today, fortunately it is another story. The community is vibrant, self-confident, active and possibly on the rise. Community members both old and young, feel we need to raise our profile. Because of our insignificant numbers, we often get overlooked.

Today, prospects seem bright, really bright, more and more youngsters are learning Hebrew and are keen about the religion.

Many elders are taking interest in coaching the youngsters in Hebrew and the tenets of Judaism.

The Jewish community, especially in Mumbai, is ripe for a resurgence of Jewish life and activity and with global inter connectedness, it is up to all of us to make it happen because global inter connectedness makes things easier to happen.

❑ ❑ ❑

Monument to the Bene Israel
Ancestors at Nawgaon

This memorial was built in 1964. The project for making a monument at Nawgaon and how this project was initiated makes for an interesting story. The Government of Maharashtra offered to build a public water reservoir in the town of Talla, provided its citizens would raise Rs 96,000/- as part funding towards the cost of construction. The fifty members of the Bene Israel congregation of the Knesset Israel Synagogue of Talla managed to raise Rs 16,000/-, one sixth of the money that had to be raised by all the residents of Talla. They contributed this amount to the authorities. Subsequently, to show their appreciation for this splendid contribution by the congregation of the Knesset Israel Synagogue, the other residents wanted to erect a suitable memorial at Talla, for them.

Grave stones marking the site where the ancestors were buried,
taken in 2000.

Taken at the site of the memorial in 1985.
(R to L: George, Akiv and me at the back).

However, the Bene Israel congregation offered another suggestion, an alternative, requesting their help in the erection of a monument to their ancestors at Nawgaon. This struck a responsive cord. Donations were collected and though everything lagged behind the original schedule, ultimately things fell into place.

All the Bene Israels made a concerted effort to construct a monument at Nawgaon in memory of their ancestors, lest posterity forget their story. Bene Israels within as well as from outside India supported the project and sent donations. A lot of non-Jews like the residents of Talla gave donations. A committee was formed under the sponsorship of the Tiphereth Israel Synagogue in Mumbai (Bombay), chaired by Mr Shellim Samuel, Advocate High Court, with representatives from all the Bene Israel synagogues and prayer halls in Bombay, Thane, Poona (Pune), Talla, Alibagh, Revdanda and others. Their first meeting was held on 19th August 1973.

The aim of the memorial project was not only to construct an impressive monument but also to provide a proper road leading up to the cemetery, put up a proper sign board and getting the road renamed after the Nawgaon cemetery, with proper fencing and providing a rest house near the cemetery. The committee also proposed to approach the Archeological Society of India and enter into an agreement for the preservation of the cemetery and get it recognized as a monument of historical significance.

The design for the monument was created by a Bene Israel architect, late Joshua Benjamin of Delhi. The design is based on the traditional Jewish symbol, the shield of David (a six pointed star), which would be the base of the six-sided pillar about 17 feet high. Appropriate Hebrew, English, Marathi inscriptions were to be written on the sides of the pillar to commemorate the landing of the first group of Bene Israels at Nawgaon. The base of the pillar was to have six black Kaddapa stones on which donor names would appear.

By 1985, though the monument was complete, due to lack of funds the peripheral wall around the cemetery could not be built nor is it built till today i.e. up to 2016. As of today, everything is in shambles, there is no peripheral wall and the monument is in a dilapidated state requiring urgent repairs. The wordings are faded and cannot be read properly. Currently, the cemetery is being used for burials and is being maintained to the some extent by the committee of the Magen Aboth Synagogue in Alibagh.

The Jerusalem Gate, Taken in 2009.

Taken in 2014, note the condition of the monument.

The Bene Israel congregation of Jerusalem built the Jerusalem gate. When I asked one of the committee members of the Magen Aboth Synagogue as to why it was named Jerusalem Gate, since the name did not seem appropriate or relevant, nor did it make any sense, he got livid, really, really angry. He told me that nobody took permission or consulted the managing committee and just did it on their own, hurting their sentiments, as if it all belonged to them only.

I asked a few non-Jewish villagers in and around that area as to what was their reaction to the entire project. Most told me that they were happy with the fact that a memorial to the Bene Israel ancestors had been built. But not a single person was happy about the naming, position and design of the gate . They said that this is Maharashtra, in India and represents the Bene Israels of Maharashtra. So it should have been named accordingly. I asked them what name would they have liked, the unanimous reply was Nawgaon Gate.

The following photographs were taken in January 2014.

Plaques----------

The Bene Israels made a concerted effort to construct a monument at Nawgaon in memory of their ancestors lest posterity forget the story.

This memorial to the ancestors of the Bene Israels of India was built in 1964 by the Bene Israels from donations received from the members of the community.

Jerusalem Gate - donations to the tune of Rs 65,000/- from the Indian Jewish Congregation of Jerusalem courtesy Mr. Noah Massil Jerusalem C.O.I.J. Israel.

Eliyahu Hannabi
Cha Tapa

---- AT KHANDALA. 20 TO 25 KMS FROM ALIBAGH.

Literally means foot prints of horses. Supposedly, there are chariot marks and in front of it 4 to 5 horse's footprints.

Legend has it that it is a place of Biblical significance. The Jews or let us say mainly the Bene Israels believe that prophet Elijah ascended to heaven on his chariot from this spot. Marks of the chariot wheels and of the hooves of the horses, about 4 or 5, can be seen on the rock at Khandala.

The first time I saw it was in 1985. At that time, there was nothing there. There was a small stream flowing and on the rocks by the side of the stream these marks are visible, though not clearly.

In the veranda of the nearest house, a chandelier for placing oil lamps, a place where the Bene Israels say the Eliyahu Hannavi prayers.

A sign board on the road indicating the site.

After the 1990's the place has been commercialized. Houses have come up next to it and the owners made rooms where Bene Israels could stay. People started having Malida there. All the ingredients were made available, but at a price. One could also get kosher food and cook it there. On the side of the rock there is a small alcove carved into the rock, where the Bene Israels light candles.

I have been there several times and observed the changes.

The chariot marks on the centre with
the horse's hoof marks on the sides.

Over the years, besides the Jews, I noticed symbols of Hinduism, the kumkum and haldi. The Hindus believe Lord Ram ascended to heaven in his chariot along with his wife Sita. Another belief is that Lord Krishna ascended to heaven on his chariot. So now it is not only the Jews, but also the Hindus who visit the site in large numbers. All this I have seen happen in a span of about 30 years. What is the real truth, I do not know.

❑ ❑ ❑

Synagogues in General

In the days of the old, the concept of congregational prayers did not exist. Worship was in the form of sacrifices, which were both animal such as goat, sheep, oxen, camels etc, birds such as chicken, ducks etc, as well as agricultural products such as sheaves of rice, wheat, barley, millet etc. at harvest time.

The Jerusalem Temple as it was then called, was just a hall with an inner Sanctum Sanctorum for the High Priests or Sanhedrin. Outside the synagogue doors, was a huge fire which had to be kept constantly burning (24 hours) for the sacrifices, as people came from far and near, at any time, even at odd times to offer their sacrifices, at their own convenience. Hence, the fire had to be kept burning, night and day, constantly burning. This was the original Ner Tamid.

Traditional prayer books contain several references to the ancient system of sacrificial practices in the Temple of Jerusalem. Some like Ezehu Mekoman and Pittum Haketoret, are legal selections from the

Talmud, which were included in the service both to recall the ancient ritual and to express the Jewish concept of study as a mode of divine worship.

The most important section of the service dealing with sacrifices is the Mussaf or additional prayers, the central theme of which deals with animal offerings. It is formulated differently for Sabbath (Tikkanta Sabbath), Rosh Hodesh (Roshai Hadashim l'Amkha Natata), the Sabbath of Rosh Hodesh (Ata Y'tzarta) and for the festivals (Umipnay Hata'enu). They all begin with references to the elaborate sacrificial system in vogue in the ancient temple in Jerusalem and voice a plea that the scattered household of Israel be reunited and the ancient ritual of sacrifice be reestablished.

Animal offerings were not only the central feature of public worship in all ancient religions contemporary with Judaism, but they also marked a great advancement over human sacrifice which was widely practiced and against which Judaism alone protested in antiquity. That the sacrificial system in the Temple did not stifle true religious fervor is borne out by the fact that it coincided with the composition of the world's most exalted religious poetry, the book of Psalms. However, the prophets and sages of Israel, whose message has been reinforced by 2000 years of history, have taught us to recognize that sincere prayers, life long study and righteous living constitute the highest form of service to God.

Hence, for many if not most Jews today, these prayers are reminiscent of Israel's ancient glory, rather than a plea for the future restoration of sacrifices. In order to make this concept more explicit, the traditional text of Tikkanta Sabbath and Umipnay Hata'em have been slightly modified. The traditional Amida also contains a brief reference to the institution of sacrifice in Retzah. "Restore the sanctuary to the sacred shrine and the fire offerings of Israel and its prayers accept in favor." This prayer is a re-adaptation of the ancient formula recited by the priest when sacrifices were offered in the temple. A medieval Midrash interpreted the phrase "the fire offerings of Israel" as referring to the martyrs of Israel who died for God's cause.

Our prayer books delete the words "the fire offerings of Israel", thus clarifying the meanings of Retzeh for modern Jews as a daily reaffirmation of their hope for the re-establishment of the religious centre of Judaism in the land of Israel.

Over a period of time, maybe hundreds of years and for various reasons, probably economical, they thought it was wastage or whatever of good food, the fire size diminished, it became smaller because people started offering only token sacrifices as that was the only form of worship.

Gradually, the learned amongst them slowly introduced reading from the five books of Moses, small passages and also introduced personal prayers. Every individual chose his or her own words to address the creator. Most people followed a standard format, sort of. Initially it was praise for God, followed by asking him for one's own needs, followed by prayers of gratitude for all that the almighty had done, both individually and collectively. Also, prayers did not include any specific timings, nor was there any codified text.

Gradually, collective prayers were introduced where the wise and learned amongst them, read from the scriptures that constituted mainly the five books of Moses. More and more people started learning to read the scriptures. The reading, which was initially said individually, gradually involved the family and then slowly, close relatives. Families and close relatives got together for the prayers, which gradually increased in numbers, until congregational prayers were introduced.

As focus changed and importance was given to the prayers, sacrifices reduced and over a period of time, they remained only symbolic. The small fire was then brought inside and placed before the Hechal—a cupboard where the five books of Moses are kept, as scrolls or as books themselves.

Again, over a period of time, scanning may be several hundreds of years, the fire was replaced by an oil lamp and placed before the Hechal. This continued to be called Ner Tamid, meaning, the light that is kept constantly burning. The Ner Tamid was kept initially to one side of the Hechal. As the oil lamp was introduced, it was placed in front of the Hechal and then carried to the twelve o'clock position for convenience.

The Hechal contains the five books of Moses, which are read over the year and they have acquired special meaning. They were placed in the Temple, later referred to as a Synagogue, in a specially made wooden cupboard or alcove called the Hechal.

Later on, these books were copied and written on parchment that had to be kept as scrolls, not in the form of a book, as the parchment would crack. Books would have to be written on paper. These scrolls were covered and kept in the Hechal and were called the Sefer Torah. Over the years, as prayers took on new meanings and the significance of the Sefer Torah was established, the scrolls were kept in the Hechal, in various types of containers, wooden, metal etc. and they were decorated as per the local tastes and designs prevalent in various parts of the world.

In some places, the five books of Moses were also printed and kept in the form of a big book that was placed in the Hechal.

Initially, only the High Priest i.e. the Sanhedrin went into the Sanctum Sanctorum to recite the prayers, but as more and more people got involved and were used to reciting the prayers themselves, in the hall of the temple now called the Synagogue, chairs and benches were placed in the hall, so they could recite the prayers more comfortably.

Often, there were differences as to which prayers should be said and by whom. This issue was resolved by Ezra (The Scribe, The Rabbi) who together with an assembly of 120 prophets and sages, established a standard text for the prayers in Hebrew. They also instituted three times for daily prayers, morning, afternoon and night.

By the second century AD, the prayers as we know them today were formulated. This is in addition to the personal, heartfelt prayers and conversations we are all encouraged to constantly initiate with God.

What form of worship took place amongst the ancestors of the Bene Israels is not clearly documented. They had lost all their prayer books and religious relics in the shipwreck and later on, in trying to make a life for themselves over hundreds of years, they forgot the language of their land, which also included the prayers. They only remembered the Sheema.

Tradition also has it that the Bene Israels observed the major Biblical festivals at approximately the right time though in a rather crude fashion. But after the arrival of David Rahabi, they added the other festivals that were instituted later, after they left their homeland, namely Hannukah. David Rahabi was instrumental in getting the Bene Israels in contact with modern Judaism.

As congregational prayers were introduced, Synagogues were built with chairs and benches for the members.

This probably happened after the Diaspora and hence the Bene Israels were not aware of it, as they had left their homeland much earlier. They started to build synagogues from the 17th century onwards.

The scattered nature of the Bene Israel population in the villages determined the form that the religious observances took, which again was mainly at the residences as home rituals. As awareness grew, congregational prayers were held at the residence of the leading family of the village especially if there was a sizable Bene Israel population, as it was later seen in the military cantonments.

In Judaism, the synagogue is seen as more than just a physical building. It is central to Jewish life and a very important institution for expression of Jewish identity, customs and traditions embedded into the social fabric of the Jewish community.

The evolution of the synagogues had gradually begun in India with rudimentary congregational recitation of the prayers when the synagogue was introduced to them for the first time as a full blown institution, because so far, they had not participated in the historic evolution of the synagogues, its scholarly and instructional functions. The Bene Israel synagogues were limited in their teaching, how to read without discussion and study. But the Bene Israel synagogues were secure in their firm foundation based on the simple faith of its congregants and their strong sense of ethnicity and separateness of their religion.

It is believed that no Jewish community is alone, each light no matter how differently it burns in each Jewish home, is connected and the pain of the dying flame affects every Jew.

Faith has long inspired some of the most remarkable synagogue architectures around the world. The Tobar synagogue in Syria, which is more than 2000 years old, is one of the most beautiful synagogues in the world even today. Recently in August 2014, it was partially damaged by the ISIS. The government of Syria has promised to repair the damages caused by the bombing. The architecture of some of the synagogues the world over are something we need to be proud of.

The premises of the Bene Israel synagogues and prayer halls are never solely used for the purpose of worship. They served and still do serve as venues for social events, a meeting place for the congregation or as a place just for idle chats, as overnight shelters for out of the town people, community administrative offices, bulletin boards and a place where children are taught how to read Hebrew and chant the prayers.

Each synagogue property is held by a trust and each trust is registered under the Bombay Public Trust Act 1950.

A very noticeable religious revival among the Bene Israel community came about in 1796, when the first synagogue in Bombay was built. It was the first occasion when they united in congregational prayers ever since they left their motherland.

The first synagogue was built by Samaji Hassaji Divekar. Various documents relate to the story of Samaji Hasaji Divekar and of his establishing the first Bene Israel Synagogue in India.

In the letter of 1768, writer and receiver of the letter not known, a Bene Israeli, again whose name is not known, stayed in Cochin for 4 years, mastering Jewish laws and regulations. This information was revealed by the Cochinis themselves. Which means that, at that point in time the Bene Israels were already aware of an institution referred to as a synagogue.

In 1767 Sultan Hyder Ali attacked Travancore and arrived at Parur which is a 6 hour journey from Cochin. The Jews of Cochin were afraid for their synagogue. Rav Ezekiel Rahabi sent his sons David, Eliahu and Moshe along with Rav Isaac Sargon to meet the Sultan and presented him with a lot of gifts. There they met Samuel who was by then released by Hyder Ali. He went with them to Cochin and saw their synagogue. Then and there, he decided to build a synagogue in Bombay after retirement. In Cochin, he came to know about the Bene Israel person who had stayed in Cochin for 4 years to study Judaism.

Samuel got a lot of promotions in the army and after retirement, as he had promised himself, built the synagogue at his own expense in 1796. After building the synagogue, he went to Cochin to procure a Sefer Torah. Just before he was to leave for home, he fell ill and died in Cochin itself. His grave is in Cochin.

The Divekar family had donated a lot of property to the synagogue, the income from which, went towards the upkeep of the synagogue, real far thinking in terms of economics, ensuring proper upkeep in the future.

Hierarchy was hereditary in those days, but only towards the male offsprings. So, having a male child was sort of mandatory. Samaji Hassaji had two wives and two daughters, but no son. After his death, his wives adopted his brother's son David who became Dada Commandan and who also became the headman or Mukkadam of the community. He served the community for the entire period of his life, in spite of ugly fractionalism within the community, for 45 years until his death in 1846. In his time, the synagogue became rich. He tried to maintain strict morality and discouraged the keeping of non-Jewish women by Bene Israel men.

The leadership was hereditary and the period from 1796 – 1886 was known as the "Commandan Rule", during which the synagogue flourished and prospered. Dada's descendnts however, mismanaged the synagogue's affairs and finances, resulting in a decline in the finances and administration.

At that point in time, Jews from Cochin, Surat, Baghdad and other places came to Bombay, giving the Bene Israels opportunities for learning more and more about their religion.

Cochini Jews took the Bene Israels closer to mainstream Judaism. The Yemenite influences were also there because of the Bene Israels staying in Aden. Eventually, Yemenite Hazanim came to officiate in some of the Bene Israel synagogues and prayer halls even in the Konkan. The first torah Scrolls which the Bene Israels received came from Yemen via Aden.

The first Torah Scroll was obtained by the second Bene Israel synagogue, not the first that was built in Bombay, i.e. the Shaare Rason Synagogue. This newly formed separate congregation in 1844 acquired the Torah Scroll as a gift from Abraham Issaji Galsurkar, a Bene Israel surveyor in Aden. Samaji's synagogue got a Torah Scroll in 1847. They received the Torah Scroll although they could not read them.

With the evolution of the synagogues through the centuries, gradually, rudimentary congregational recital of prayers was introduced to the Bene Israels, because they had not participated in the historic evolution of the synagogues, its scholarly and instructional functions. They found it difficult to read the Torah as the Hebrew letterings were without vowels. The Bene Israel synagogues were limited in their teaching about how to read with discussion and study.

The Kazis helped organize the congregations of the synagogues. They helped appoint a leader of the congregation who was called a Mukkadam (meaning leader), who was assisted by 4 or 5 elderly counselors called Choglas. Then there was a Gabbai (treasurer), a Hazan (reader), who was either a Cochini or a Yemenite Jew and who also sometimes performed the duties of a Shohet, Mohel and Sopher (teacher). Then there was also a Shamash (caretaker) who also functioned as a source of information about the community members. The Jamat or the Assembly of the congregants, consisted of all its male members. There was no Rabbi. The administration of the synagogues was organized by the Mukkadam, assisted by the Choglas This group was known as the Mankaris (dignitaries) who regulated the life of the Bene Israels.

The Mukkadam selected all the cadres except the Shamash, who was selected by the Jamat i.e. the congregation. Only the Hazan, Clerk and the Shamash received salaries, all the other posts were honorary. This system exists even today, only the nomenclature has changed. The congregation selects a president, a secretary and a treasurer, with an office clerk who could be a non-Jew and a caretaker who could also be a non-Jew. The office of the Mukkadam was hereditary. Till today the Hazan, Shamash and Clerk receive bonuses on Rosh ha Shana.

In some cases, Hazzanim from the Bagdadi Jewish community of Bombay led the prayer services in the Bene Israel synagogues. Recently, in addition to the earlier influences, a few European Ashkenazi melodies have become a part of the Bene Israel religious practice.

One peculiar custom of the Bene Israels is the bidding in the synagogues, for opening of the Hechal, for carrying of the Sefer Torah, reading the Torah i.e. the portions of the Torah i.e. Shenies, also certain important prayers etc. The logic being that, it is a source of income for the synagogue.

It is important to note that the Bene Israel synagogues and prayer halls all over the Konkan at one time numbered 300 and today, especially in the small towns and villages, they are practically extinct. This is because of the mass immigration to Israel and elsewhere, which was much more from the Konkan initially and later on mass exodus even from the cities in the late 1960's to the first half of 1970's.

The rural Bene Israel congregations are too small to maintain their local synagogues, even though there is still sufficient income coming in from the synagogue land holdings which are rented out to tenant farmers. There are very few worshippers at each synagogue. In some synagogues, especially in the smaller villages with not much of land holdings and with very little income coming in, they find it very difficult to pay the taxes due on the synagogue, land and properties, although the synagogue itself is exempt from taxes. In several cases however, the remaining few Bene Israels in the villages do not agree to sell the synagogues or its properties, since doing so would deprive them of the synagogue which is so dear to them even if they are too few to even constitute a minyan.

Even so, it is heartening to see that several youngsters who must have emigrated with their parents as children or maybe even as teenagers, many of them come back, off and on, on visits to the synagogues, get it painted, polish the benches, chairs, tables and the teba and say the prayers there whenever they come visiting.

In many villages which I visited, these youngsters pay a lump sum amount of money to a care taker, getting him / her to look after the synagogue, its cleanliness and light the lamp in front of the Hechal, although there may be nothing there, no books, no Sefer Torah, nothing. In some places they ask the care-taker to light the Sabbath candles and teach them the prayers for lighting the candles/ oil lamps. In India, as far as religion goes, once entrusted, mostly, they fulfill their commitment or they will not take up the job itself. Of course this may not be so in all cases.

Talking to several people both Jews and non-Jews, I was given to understand that practically every village in the Konkan had Bene Israels living there and they had either a small synagogue or a prayer hall. Let me put it this way, wherever there were Bene Israels living, could be just a few families, even less than a total of ten, they always had a synagogue or a prayer hall. In some smaller villages, the synagogues were just mud walls with a thatched roof, which often had to be rebuilt / repaired because of the weather conditions.

The Bene Israels were quite devout. They observed the Sabbath, kept Kashruth and celebrated all the festivals. Wherever there was no synagogue, people from the surrounding villages would attend prayers in the larger synagogue. For Yom Kippur, on Erev Kippur, they would have their meals, light the lamp in their homes and walk to the synagogue where they wanted to attend the prayers. They would come home only after the prayers were over the next day after sunset and after breaking their fast. Most people would sleep in the synagogue itself or in the house of members who lived within walking distance from the synagogue. There was a Thalkar family who had a huge house, enough to accommodate about fifty people. Several families came together, all cooked and ate together and then attended the services in the synagogues. Very commendable!

They observed the local custom of removing one's shoes, slippers or sandals before entering the house or a holy place, which in their case was the synagogue. Since footwear is made of leather and is taboo in holy places, so also they observed it in the synagogues. There was always a well built on one side, where they would first wash their hands and feet after removing their footwear and then enter the synagogue.

The wells are still very much a part of the synagogues in the Konkan areas, but most are today covered and not in use. Taps have replaced them, which are strategically placed on one side of the entrance, usually on the left, where members wash their hands and feet before entering the synagogue. This custom is strictly followed even today. So this custom of removing one's footwear before entering is still strictly followed in the Konkan synagogues before entering, whether it for prayers or just a casual visit . In fact, in all the Bene Israel synagogues in India, this custom is still observed on Yom Kippur and Tisha Be Ab.

In case a village had a small prayer hall, or a very tiny synagogue, with not much of surrounding land for a well, at the entrance and to one side, a bucket or any container filled with water was always kept where the worshippers would first wash their hands and feet before entering the synagogue.

Most villages had their own graveyards. Some of the very small villages shared the graveyards of the neighboring villages. Some graveyards are still in use. Few are well kept, most are not, and some have graves dating back to 1600 to most recent times. Some gravestones are well preserved and show the dates, names etc clearly, although very old. Most gravestones are broken and the words cannot be read. Many graves I saw date back to 1760 or even earlier. I want to mention one graveyard at Gondhalpada, located on the road to Alibagh from Kihim, wherein there were several graves dating 1739, 1750 and one dated 1670. Names and other details were however not clearly visible.

There is a second graveyard close by, in fact there itself, just next door, but there are Muslim graves on one side too. Probably there is no one to object, so it has been taken over by the Muslims.

The Bene Israel cemeteries outside the Konkan:

In Maharashtra - Ahmednagar, Dissa, Kampti, Lonavla, Mhaow, Nagpur, Panchgani, Pune, Satara and Solapur.

In Gujarat - Ahmedabad, Baroda, Rajkot and Surat.

In Madhya Pradesh - Jabalpur.

In Rajasthan - Ajmer.

In New Delhi - Vijapur

As there were Bene Israels settled there, according to Ezekiel Rahabi who wrote that there are Jews in India at Vijapur and they are called Bene Israels and they are scattered in all the Maratha towns.

By the second century BC, the prayers as we know them today were formulated. This is in addition to the personal, heartfelt prayers and conversations we are all encouraged to constantly initiate with the Almighty.

So starts the history of the Bene Israel synagogues in India. In this book I will be dealing only with the synagogues in the Konkan area.

With each synagogue in the Konkan, I shall try to give the history, background and several anecdotes and experiences I encountered on my visits to the synagogues, their evolution over the years and as seen by me while visiting some of the synagogues as a child and my memories of those synagogues. Then, visiting several synagogues as an adult several times and documenting them as seen by me specifically 15 years back, then again in 2014 and as recently as 2015, documenting their state of affairs then and now with photographs wherever possible.

Synagogues in the KONKAN

I - BETH EL Synagogue; Revdanda, Alibagh Taluka.

The name of the synagogue means 'House of God'.

The synagogue from the front.
(Taken in 2005.)

George blowing the Shofar in the synagogue, 2005.

Plaques on the outer wall, 2005.

The synagogue's first establishment was mainly due to the effort's of Hacham Shellomo Salem Shurrabi (mentioned earlier).

The Bene Israels of Revdanda claim that this was the first synagogue to be built in the Raigad district. It was originally built in 1842 and was rebuilt in 1876. Construction costs were met because of voluntary donations and contributions. An extension i.e. the ladies gallery was built in 1877. The centenary of the synagogue was celebrated on Sunday 28th December 1948.

A temporary synagogue was built in 1840 only for the pensioned troops of the British, who gave them land in the cantonment area. It was a temporary or make shift structure, not built of stone and concrete. Hence it was subject to weather conditions. It was rebuilt in 1842, during the British and Portuguese rule. At that point in time, there were 35 to 40 Bene Israel families living in Revdanda and the surrounding villages.

The synagogue was well managed, initially by Samuel Jacob Dandekar and the congregation. They never had any major fights and splits in the old days, in fact this system exists even today.

Many Bene Israels worked in the Revdanda and Corley fort and palaces. In the forts and palaces, several plaques are still there which give evidence of the presence of the Bene Israels. They worked in administration, keeping accounts etc, as well as in the army as fighters. The highest rank they could earn was Subedar Major.

The trust board members have buried their old dilapidated Sefer Torahs on the side of the synagogue, which is marked by a stone and is on one side where no one ventures.

The synagogue as seen from the side, 2014.

The front of the synagogue, the entrance door, 2014.

The ladies gallery as seen from inside the synagogue, 2014.

In 2012, renovation work in the form of only repairs and painting was carried out . At present only 10 families live in and around Revdanda.

Previously, Mr. Isaac Shapurkar, a tailor by profession and a trust board member looked after the maintenance, collection of funds and administrative work. The prayers were said by Mr. Isaac Ghosalkar, who was assisted by Mr Benjamin Waskar who has a furniture shop.

As of now, Mr Benjamin Waskar of Theronda, Revdanda looks after the synagogue. He says the prayers in the synagogue, in fact acts as the Chazzan, Mohel and Shohet, in fact everything rolled into one.

His father sent him to learn Hebrew and all the various prayers from the hazzans of all the synagogues in Mumbai. He also learnt to become a Mohel and a Shohet at the ORT Mumbai. Now, he renders his services to several people, not only in Revdanda and the surrounding villages, but also to the Jews living in far-off places such as Pen, Panvel, Apta and many more. He does not charge any personal fees for his services, only the synagogue charge of Rs 501/- and the bus fare. He is doing yeoman service to the people, indeed a great mitzvah.

I found him to be sincere, dedicated and a real social worker. He runs his own business, but devotes a lot of time for the synagogue activities, as well as catering to the needs of the Bene Israels day and night.

This synagogue is well maintained, the funds are maintained and utilized properly for the upkeep of the synagogue. The synagogue is surrounded by a huge wada, which has a large number of coconut and betel nut trees, a good source of revenue. There is a well to the back and on one side, which has been covered, as it is no longer used. The wada is also looked after well. As a visitor, if you give a donation, you are given a proper receipt.

Mr. Benjamin Waskar says the prayers in the synagogue daily. If he is out, one of his son's steps in and says the prayers. It is the only synagogue in the Konkan, where prayers are said daily. For Friday and Saturday services, there are approximately 6 gents. For the festivals, there are about 15 people.

He teaches Hebrew to a number of youngsters including his own two sons, who also help out in the prayers. He looks to the future, ensuring that the prayers will continue in this synagogue. Four boys whom he had taught Hebrew and trained them in all aspects of the religion had their Bar Mitzvah (Aliyah to the Torah) in the Revdanda synagogue. Recently one of his own sons had his Bar Mitzvah.

This synagogue has its own graveyard which is about a hundred years old.

View from the synagogue door to the outside showing the various palm trees, 2014.

Plaques outside the synagogue.

Mrs. Naomi and Mr. Ezriel Rahamim Penkar - Expenses towards flooring work of Synagogue, in loving memory of his parents late Mrs. Esther and late Mr. Rahamim Solomon Penkar in the year 2008.

Plaque at the bottom.

This place is dangerous. This is only the Lord's house, the gateway to Heaven. Donated by Sarabai Awaskar in memory of her son Ishak Shalomji.

II - Magen Aboth Synagogue - Alibagh Taluka Alibagh.

The name of this synagogue means 'The Shield of Father'. According to the locals, it means 'Land of the Elders'.

Address: Israel Aali, Shivalkar Naka, Alibagh, District Raigad, 402201.

Alibagh was first called Angria Kulaba.

George at the entrance door to the synagogue, 2000.

Entrance gate - taken in 2000

The Teba.

The entrance gate,
2005.

Entrance to the synagogue
after renovations, taken in 2005.

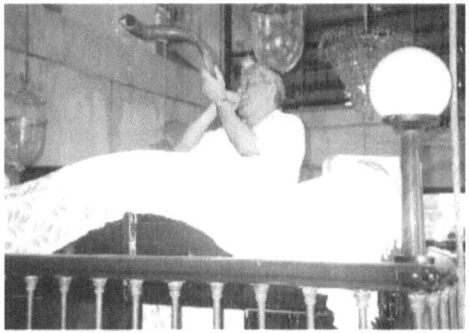

George blowing the shofar, 2005.

The ladies gallery, 2005.

Interiors of the
synagogue taken in 2005.

When the synagogue was built at Alibagh, there was a lot of disharmony amongst the members of the congregation. Hacham Shellomo Salem Shurrabi did his level best to improve the conditions prevalent in the synagogue, but to no avail. His efforts however deserve praise.

This synagogue was first built by the English servicemen for the Jewish pensioners in 1840. But the synagogue was small, so it was rebuilt in 1848and then again in 1910, through voluntary contributions. Many claim that this was the first synagogue to be built in Raigad district in 1840. However, the present building was built in 1910 by the Bene Israels who gave generously towards the synagogue funds. It was inaugurated on 25th December 1910 with great pomp and revelry. On that occasion the synagogue was named "Magen Aboth".

After being built in 1910, for 50 years no repairs were carried out, they claim that no repairs were required. Then slowly they noticed that repairs were required, but again no major repairs were carried out, that is why during the rains leakages developed but still no repairs were carried out.

The synagogue celebrated its golden jubilee on the 15th May 1960, when more than 1000 people participated. Earlier the Bene

Israels from the surrounding villages like Thal, Akshi, Nagoan, Revdanda, Saswane, Dighordy, Kihim and Nogaon would attend prayers in this synagogue.

In the 1950s, 1960s and early 1970s, there was mass migration of Jews to Israel and the congregation in Magen Aboth dwindled. Up to 1950 there were about 100 people in Alibagh. The numbers slowly declined. Just seven families live in Alibagh today, but for the High Holy days, people come from the surrounding villages.

There is an interesting story of the family of Banaji Wakrulkar. His son Simon Benjamin Wakrulkar was born in 1841. Later on in life he became a famous writer. He has written about various incidents that occurred in the synagogue. As a child he used to go for prayers to the synagogue along with his father. He had also been taught Hebrew. As a child, on one occasion when he went for prayers, he was standing next to his father, sidur in his hand and was trying to cope up with the prayers that the congregation were reciting / singing. He missed some lines. His father corrected him. Again he missed some lines and again his father corrected him. This happened 2 – 3 times, but he kept on missing lines. Finally his father got so exasperated that in front of the entire community present in the synagogue, he slapped him hard twice. The son though small felt terribly humiliated, besides having red cheeks. Rubbing his cheeks he ran home, and after that he never ever went to the synagogue.

This incident happened to him at a very tender age, but it looks like he never forgot it. As an adult when he became a writer, he wrote a book titled "Mulanna Dillai Zaranya Sharirik Shikha", meaning, 'Children being given physical punishments'. A second book "Shikshenene Mulay Sudhartath", meaning 'Children improve with education'. With both these books he wanted to show the elders, that if you physically beat children, they get worse. He advocated that, teach children with love and care and see how they flourish. He expressed those feelings at that point in time and made a lot of effort to teach people that. He went from school to school, putting forth his thoughts, very progressive for that age. He received a number of awards for his books and his thoughts. He made a lot of good changes not only for the community, but also for society at large.

Not only that, he sent his wife Rebeccabai to the Grant Medical College to study midwifery, following which she spent her whole life in the service of the community and the rest of the population. She wrote books on women's diseases, and how they should take care of themselves and their children. She studied Gujarati and wrote a number of articles on health in the newspaper published by the Angrias called "Sudharak" which was quite famous. She was felicitated by the rulers for that. She was a great inspiration for the women of that time. She was also felicitated for her work by the Maharaja of Baroda (Vadodara is its new name) Sayajirao Gaikwad.

From the beginning, the synagogue always had good hazans. After the Yom Kippur prayers, they would give Mish Barakha not only to the families of those present for the prayers, but they would also give blessings to the Royal family members. This tradition is still followed in most of the Bene Israel synagogues in India even today, where we confer blessings on the respective state heads like the Governor, Chief Minister and the State Ministers as well as the national heads like the President, Prime Minister and the Union Ministers.

There is another custom amongst the Bene Israels, they visit relatives and friends after Yom Kippur. In Alibagh, the Jews would also visit the Royal family. They visited the Angrais in their darbar and again conferred blessings. The Angrais always welcomed them in their darbar.

On Jewish festivals, from the Harikot fort in Alibagh, the Angrais would fire canons and wish the Bene Israels. For Simhath Torah, the Angrais would send baskets of flowers and boxes of sweetmeats (mithai) to the synagogue. They lived with the others as one.

It was during the reign of Kanoji Angrai, that in the Durbar, he changed the name "Shanivar Teli" to Bene Israel. He used to attend a number of Bene Israel functions. During his reign, he gifted Samaji and Abaji Charikar a lot of land in appreciation of their services and conferred them with the title of 'Naik Mukkadom'.

The Alibagh fort was an honorable place for the Bene Israel men. In that fort a lot of Bene Israel men worked as care takers and they were so good at their jobs that later on they were named as Killekar, Gadkar and Bhorapkar. The words killa, gad, and bhorap, all mean fort in Marathi.

After that era, many Bene Israels migrated to Bombay (Mumbai). Many retained their houses in Alibagh. For the festivals, they all came to Magen Aboth, their own synagogue for the prayers.

Another Bene Israel from Alibagh who did extremely well was Solomon Moses Wakrulkar, who was born in 1909. I believe as a child he studied under a lamp-post, as there was no electricity at his residence. He had to overcome a lot of hardships to reach his goal of becoming a solicitor and shifted his base to Bombay and fought his first case in the Bombay High Court. He was the first Bene Israel Solicitor in India. Also, Aaron Shapurkar of Alibagh did a lot of work for various synagogues.

The Bene Israels of Alibagh had flour mills of both rice and wheat, soda water factories and oil presses.

The state of the synagogue slowly deteriorated and the condition was really bad. Cement and paint was falling , water was seeping into the synagogue during the rains and also into the Eliyahu Hannabi light. Levi Bhonkar and Abraham Awaskar made tremendous efforts with backing from their wives to complete the work.

When Levi Bhonkar was the president and Jacob Isaac Awaskar was secretary, they would take their children before the festivals to clean the synagogue, wipe the floors, clean the benches, wash the glass hundies, make the oil lamps and get everything spic and span before the start of the prayers. I think it is really creditable.

On the 24th of July 2000 on Tisha Be Ab at 1.30 am, due to torrential rains, a portion of the external plaster of the front wall of the synagogue became loose, resulting in the detachment of the marble tablets of the Ten Commandments, which were fixed there in 1910. It fell to the ground and broke into several pieces. This shook the community and they were all the more determined to care for and preserve their heritage.

With the help of donations from India, Israel, USA and many other countries, the synagogue building was repaired, painted and two new marble tablets, with the Ten Commandments engraved in gold letterings were reaffixed on the synagogue wall above the entrance door. The renovation was celebrated at its 93rd Anniversary on 28th December 2003 where several hundred people attended.

The centenary celebrations were held on 26th December 2010.

The first time I attended services in the Alibagh Synagogue, as we used to call it, was when I was about 8 years old. Then there was no electricity. On Friday evening for the services, the synagogue was lit by a number of oil lamps put in the chandeliers. When the welcome song to the Shabbat bride i.e. Lekha Dodhi was being sung, it gave a very fairytale like feeling in the synagogue. All the chandeliers were lit by oil lamps and the congregation was singing gustily. The whole atmosphere was so enchanting for me coming from Bombay, where there was electricity. I can still visualize that scene whenever I think of Friday prayers at the Alibagh synagogue.

The fairytale enchantment is gone, as electricity is in, but that moment in time has a special place in my heart and has been etched there forever.

The synagogue has a lot of space around it. There are mainly coconut palms with a few betel nut palms too. There is a well of the synagogue built to one side but today it is covered.

III - Knesset Israel Synagogue: Tala Ghosale Mangaon Taluka.

The name of the synagogue means 'Assembly of Israel'.

Outside the synagogue in 2005 – (from left) George and our friends Sophie and Moshe.

The entrance today, 2014

George and me on the side of the well,
which is to our left, 2014.

George and I, inside the synagogue with the staircase
in the background leading to the ladies gallery.

This synagogue was built in April 1849. This synagogue was destroyed by a fire in 1852 and was rebuilt. Again for the third time, it was rebuilt in 1910.

Plaque at the entrance, 2000

I first saw this synagogue in 2000 and then again in 2014. It is a one storied building. In the middle of the last century there were mainly Bene Israel residents in Tala. For the Jewish holidays, all the residents from the nearby villages such as Ghosale, Satambe, Halde, Walis, Salcette and others would walk 3 to 4 miles to the Tala synagogue arriving before sunset on the eve of the holiday spending the night at the local residences of the Bene Israel families, so that they could attend the synagogue for the entire festival service. One Thalkar family as mentioned earlier, had a huge house, big enough to accommodate fifty people. People gathered early at that house, helped and cooked together, ate together and slept there too.

It is a very small synagogue, hardly 10 by 10 feet. At the entrance on the right side is the door beyond which is the staircase leading to the ladies gallery. Facing east there is small curtained portion on the wall, more like an alcove, like a closed window covered by a curtain. The synagogue was closed, in fact it had stopped functioning in the early part of the 20th century because there were no Jews left in that area.

When I went there for the first time in 2000, opposite the synagogue we went to a home where an old Hindu couple probably in their eighties or early nineties lived. We requested the use of their toilet. Their name was Nimkar. The toilet was in the corner of a huge poorly lit room. All sorts of vegetables like pumpkins, coconuts, betel nuts etc were stored in that room. When we went there, and while we took turns to freshen up, the old lady regaled us with Sabbath songs. She knew them all by heart, the tunes, the words everything was perfect. We were really surprised and we told her that. She then told us that she came to live in that house as a young bride when she was just 6 years old. Every Friday she used to listen to the Sabbath songs and gradually she knew them by heart. She used to sing along with the congregation but in her own home.

When we came outside, both she and her husband, both toothless, sang a number of Simhath Torah songs. It was such pleasure to listen to them. We were truly mesmerized and were hoping we had some recording device with us. We sat there with them, listening to them for a real long time.

As we were leaving, they urged us to restart the prayers in the synagogue. They told us that on Fridays they sit outside their home and sing the Sabbath songs at sunset. Such faith, so true of the village people.

In 2014, when I revisited their house, the old couple I was told, are no more. I met their daughter-in-law instead. Also, the house was not the same. It was no longer a typical village house, but a new modern house with a lot of gadgets, more mod really. I felt sad about the old couple. I prayed silently and sincerely for them, praying that wherever they may be, they should be happy and that their souls should rest in peace.

When the Bene Israels of Talla left, prayers had stopped and the last few to leave had handed over the synagogue to the Zilla Parishad, who started a kindergarten there, which closed down almost immediately till 2014, when they in turn handed it over to a primary school teacher named Savita. She showed us the Hechal, which was a window sized space in the wall covered with a silken curtain, very old and discolored at places but clean. When she opened the curtain she told us that there was a huge book placed inside which she was told were the five books of Moses in one volume that was kept there.

During the torrential rains, which had ravaged the area on 26th July 2000, the book was completely soaked through and through because of the flooding. After the deluge the book was wet and moldy. After she took over the place to run a nursery, which was just three months prior to our visit, she found the book in bad shape. So every day she would wipe one page at a time carefully and then put it out to dry in the sun. Her efforts, painful but sincere, were successful and she managed to salvage the book.

Just two days before my visit, she had two visitors, one Shalom Moshe Ashtamkar and the other Moses Fansapurkar. They took the book with them. However, she made them write their names and mobile telephone numbers in a register, sign it and only then did she give them the book. She showed me the register and it was from it that I got their telephone numbers.I contacted them ,but they refused to answer any of my questions.

Every morning when she comes to the school, she cleans it up, stands before the Hechal and does a Namaskar. She also keeps the room neat and tidy. She gets the children to remove their shoes outside as she tells them it is a holy place. That day she had made peanut and jaggery cookies for the children, which she offered us too and I must say they were tasty.

I was really impressed with her. I gave Savita Rs 200/- and told her to buy something for the children to eat. I called her a week later to thank her, when she told me that she had bought Almonds and Dates and had distributed it amongst the children, telling them that the guests who had visited them had sent it for them. I asked her why almonds and dates, why not chocolates. I was extremely happy when she told me that this was healthier for the children. Her awareness and intelligence definitely requires mention.

In the tiny room of the synagogue, the mezuzah was still there, it was clean and the walls were painted. We went outside around the school and found that there was a lot of area around it. There was a well at the back on one side. The well wall was high and the well seemed deep. It was covered with palm leaves and branches of trees, so that the children do not fall into it while playing. Also the area of the school has been fenced off.

IV - Beth Ha Elohim Synagogue Pen-
(The Name Meaning "Home of God")

Tamid light, 2005.

At the entrance, 2005.

View from the side taken in 2005.

The Sefer Torah, 2005.

After the renovation, 2012

This synagogue was built in 1863, rebuilt in 1893. Prior to the building of the synagogue, a prayer hall was opened at the private residence of Jamedar Isaac Elloji Nawgaonkar, the son of a celebrated ballet singer amongst the Bene Israels Eloji. Subsequently, a prayer hall was opened at the house of late Varvatnekar Jamedar. In the meantime B. Santkel Benjamin Kandlekar donated his house and a piece of land for the building of a synagogue, which was built with the help of donations given by Hannahbai, widow of Haeem David Divekar. The synagogue was consecrated in 1863 i.e. 1st Elul 5623. It was rebuilt and rededicated on 7th March 1893. Just like the Bene Israels elsewhere, here also among the Bene Israels of Pen, jealousies resulted in various factions. But they reconciled before the synagogue needed major repairs. It was rebuilt by the people themselves through donations and rededicated on 9th March 1893. This synagogue owned about fifty acres of land, the synagogue is really well off. One of the richest synagogues in the Konkan.

Interiors after renovation, 2012

After renovation, 2012

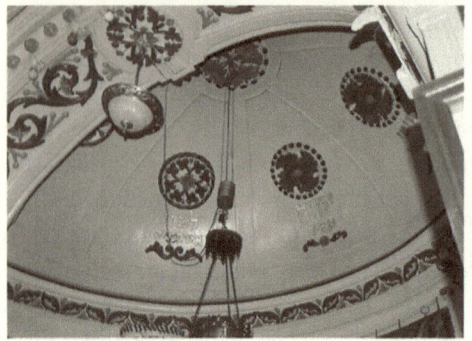

Ceiling after renovation, 2012

There was a policy of this synagogue that whoever was appointed as Hazan or Shamash was to be given free accommodation outside. The Shamash who was appointed was one Samuel Haskel Penkar, commonly referred to as Samuel baba. He joined when he was a young boy and served until his death. Both the dates, of his joining and his death, I could not ascertain. He was a very sincere, hardworking and honest Shamash. He served the synagogue till his death.

Till the early part of the 1900s, there were about 50 families in Pen. Also Bene Israel families from Kamarli, Vakrul, Kandla, Valak came to this synagogue for prayers. Once immigration started, there were only about 8-10 families left. One family from Valak, a Penkar looked after the fort of Shivaji at Valak. The oil that the Bene Israel families pressed in Valak, was supplied to Shivaji's soldiers at the fort. This Penkar family, or rather their descendants, who looked after the fort are still there but they have shifted to Pen.

Mr. Santkel Benjamin Kandlekar, who donated the land for the synagogue looked after the affairs of the synagogue till his death. After his demise, Moshe Rahamim Penkar took over. Over a period of time, his son Abraham Moshe Penkar took over. Most of the Bene Israels had rice mills, oil presses and wadas. One Abraham Moshe Penkar had rice mills and brick kilns.

In the early 1900s, most of the Bene Israels of Pen were quite well off with bungalows of their own ands were also very generous. A retired judge, Mr. Rohekar, came to stay in Pen and he was given a bungalow by Mr. Moshe Rahamim Penkar. The bungalow is still there though sold to someone else.

Either Mr. Moshe or Mr. Abraham Rahamim Penkar have given a lot of the synagogue land either on lease or have sold it, no one is sure. The family has since migrated to Israel. This is such a loss to the synagogue and the community.

When the western express highway between Mumbai and Pune was being built, Moses Abraham Penkar who worked for the RTO and now lives in Pune after retirement, met a friend/colleague one Mr. Mhatre, who informed him that 10 acres of the synagogue land near Kandla was being taken over by the government for land development. So he, along with the synagogue committee members approached the government and got compensation in the form of money, which is now put in a fixed deposit in a bank, a sort of a safe deposit.

Right now there are just 4-5 families left in Pen with no one to say the prayers. Since 2006 Ariana Oren Penkar, who is the daughter-in-law of Mr. and Mrs. Moses Abraham Penkar (RTO), said the prayers in the synagogue for the high holy days with some help from her husband Oren. However due to various problems, she discontinued in 2014.

Many Bene Israels who were residents of Pen and are now living in Israel, collected a lot of money as donations and in 2011 renovated the synagogue. The anniversary and completion of the renovation was celebrated on the 8th January 2012, when more than a 1000 people attended from India, Israel and elsewhere.

The remarkable thing about that occasion was that various people spoke and they were mostly Israelis. They spoke in Hebrew, some in Marathi and what was most impressive was that they all reminisced about the synagogue, about the prayers, Simhath Torah and all the fun they had together and also the various other fun filled festivals and occasions they used to have.

They also told us about the significance of the Pen synagogue, something to the effect that whoever prayed in the synagogue for something and got it, then they would come back to say thanks and do a malida.

There is a well on one side of the synagogue near the entrance itself. This is slightly different as compared to other synagogues in the Konkan.

V - Hesed El Synagogue;
Poynad Alibagh Taluka.

The name of synagogue means 'Bounty of God'.

This synagogue was built in 1866 and rebuilt in 1933. In 1866, the synagogue was built by local subscriptions and donations. It was named Hesed El Synagogue in 1933. This synagogue, since its inception was never in a prosperous condition.

In 2000, when I visited the synagogue, I found that it is a very small, really cute synagogue, but it had stopped functioning by the late 1800s, because there were hardly any Bene Israel residents left in Poynad.

Outside the Synagogue, 2005,
from left me Mr. Nawgavkar Standing, Moshe sitting

Mr. Nawgavkar inside the Synagogue, 2005.

The synagogue was looked after by David Nawgavkar, who owns a lot of land and horses. He trained horses to dance and perform to music. They also perform a lot of tricks. He has a knack for training horses. He hires out his horses for functions including marriages.

He lives there with his wife. Their house is exactly behind the synagogue. No prayers are said there, they only light the Ner Tamid light and the Shabbat candles in the synagogue.

In 2014, when I visited the synagogue, I was told that Mr. David Moses Nawgavkar had died in 2013. His two sons came down from Israel. His wife migrated to Israel along with her eldest son. The younger son Avidan Moses David Nawgavkar came back to Poynad in 2014. He has cleaned up the synagogue, got it painted and spruced up. It really looks good now compared to what I had seen on my earlier visits. He lights the Ner Tamid light and says the prayers in the synagogue.

Synagogue entrance, 2014.

Name of the synagogue above the entrance, 2014.

Plaque which reads: Hesed El Jewish Synagogue Poynad consecrated in the year 1866 anniversary, 1933.

Below: Interiors of the synagogue, 2014

Interiors

Avidan is building a hotel/resort called Shalom Hotel/Resort, which is very close to the synagogue and which he plans to run. He has also renovated the house i.e. his parent's house in which he plans to live.

The funny part is that when I visited in 2014, Avidan was not there but his friends who were Hindus, opened the synagogue for us, got candles for us to light in the synagogue and told us all about him and the resort. They help him regularly. It is all so amazing.

The well is behind the synagogue towards the house. The horses' stables are also behind but on the other side of the well, all now well maintained.

Plaques

1. Bene Iarael
   Kesed El
   Jewish Synagogue
   Poynad
   Established in Year 1833
   Centenary 1933
   Nutan Karen.

2. Hesed El Synagogue
   Poynad – Zilla –Kolaba
   Inauguration Ceremony
   Dated 31 December 1933.

VI - Shaarai Shalom Synagogue in Borlai.

It was previously Janjira State, now Alibagh Taluka.

Address: Borlai--- Mandla Taluka, Murud Zilla Parishad.

Plaque above the entrance, 2000.

Entrance to the compound, 2000.

That's me near the Hechal, 2000.

George blowing the Shofar, 2000.

Entrance gate, 2005.

Entrance is the synagogue

George blowing the shofar inside the synagogue, 2005.

Interiors, 2005.

Borlai is a village in Hubshi.

The name of the synagogue means 'Gates of Peace'. It was built in 1865. It was built at the personal expense of Shalom Isaac Sogavkar and was dedicated in May 1869. He also donated some land so that the income from its yields can be utilized for the expenditure of the synagogue and its upkeep. Later on for reasons unknown, it sort of closed down, probably by Michael Sogavkar. Here also there was a lot of disparity amongst the members.

Currently, Sunny Sogavkar who lives just next to the synagogue looks after it. According to him, the synagogue was actually built by Saleman Sheth who was 25 years old at that time and was his great grandfather. Shalom Isaac Sogavkar and Saleman are one and the same person.

The synagogue is 150 years old. The road from the main road up to the synagogue is called Israel Ally and the road from the main road to the house of Sunny Sogavkar is called Saleman Sheth Sogavkar road.

I have visited this synagogue five times. It is very cute and small and reminded me of a matchbox. The centenary was celebrated in 1965 on Sunday 9th May.

Earlier, when I visited the synagogue in 2000, the Hazzan was one Mr Ashtamkar. Later on Sunny's father used to say the prayers in the synagogue.

The synagogue was renovated with help from Jews and non-Jews by old man Sogavkar. From the outset, the synagogue is looked after by the Sogavkar family. Prayers were said by Sunny's father and after his death, there was no one to say the prayers and the prayers have stopped altogether.

At the present moment, there is a casing of a Sefer Torah in the Hechal, but there is no scroll. Also, there is no Tamid light. Although I have visited this synagogue 5 times, we never checked the Sefer Torah except on this last visit in 2014. George opened the Sefer Torah and found that it was empty.

Old man Sogavkar has 5 children, 3 sons and 2 daughters. One son is Sunny, who still lives in Borlai, one is in Israel and one in Pune. One daughter lives in Thane and one is in Israel. Sunny has married a Christian woman and did not seem interested in the synagogue while his father was alive.

Now the scenario is different. Sunny has started taking keen interest in the synagogue. His wife though a Christian, looks after the cleanliness of the synagogue and the compound. Their house also opens into the same compound as the synagogue.

The synagogue was recently renovated. Sunny and his siblings have decided that whatever fields and wadas are left behind as inheritance, that money will be utilized for the upkeep of the synagogue. Thus it was renovated, well painted, very clean and really cared for when I saw it in 2014. In fact I would say that it was the cleanest synagogue in the Konkan that I saw in 2014.

Today there are 7 to 8 Jewish houses in Borlai gaon and 1 family in Corley. Whenever the younger brother visits from Israel, he says the prayers in the synagogue.

Five years back Sunny renovated the synagogue again. He is doing pretty well. He has a good house, runs an ambulance service and has 3 cars that he runs as taxis. All his vehicles are parked near his house.

I suggested to Sunny that he could place a zero watt bulb in front of the Hechal, as a Tamid light, which he appreciated and decided to implement. I hope he has done so.

Plaques.

1) The renovation of the synagogue consisting of the ladies gallery, office premises and installation of electricity was achieved due the untiring efforts of the then President Shri Daniel Eliyahoo Sogavkar and Honorary Secretary and Trustee Shri Michael Eliyahoo Sogavkar by full financial co-operation of the members of the community.

2) The major collection of the donations with the help of Shri Shellim Joseph Massil (Bombay) is laudable and unforgettable. Shri Samuel David Nagavkar (Transport Contracter) Bombay and Shrimati Sarabai S Nagavkar donated Rs 1001/- in memory of Late Mr. David S Nagavkar, Late Mrs. Miriambai D Nagavkar and Late Mr. Jacob D Nagavkar.

3) This synagogue was built by Azam Shallom Ishak Sogavkar Mehter and his wife Seemabai. These two with love built it for the Jews and for this work the expenditure was Rs 1400/-. The synagogue work was finished and they were felicitated on 3rd (?) 1791.

VII - Ambepur Synagogue in Ambepur (Cheul) Alibagh Taluka.

The synagogue was built in 1868, partly at the expense of Joseph Solomon Sankar and partly by voluntary donations. It was destroyed by a fire in 1874 and was rebuilt in January 1884. Again, the synagogue was destroyed following a a storm and was rebuilt by Mr. Soloman Dighorkar, who with his family are the only residents in Ambepur. Again the synagogue was destroyed by natural calamities

Photo taken inside the synagogue in 2005.
George is pictured with Mr. Solomon Dighorkar.

The first time I visited this synagogue, as is seen in the picture above, there was only one wall with a curtain in front, a table placed in front of it with two candle stands for the Sabbath candles and at the other end i.e. supposedly the entrance, the main door, only the door was present. No walls, no roof. Soloman Dighorkar and his family comprising his mother, wife and a younger son Shellim are staying there opposite the synagogue. The son is doing BSc and one son lives in Israel. They say their Friday prayers there.

According to the Dighorkar family, there is a conflict as to the exact date when the synagogue was built. According to some sources it was built in 1874 and rebuilt in 1884. This synagogue was built partly at the expense of Joseph Solomon Sankar and partly by means of voluntary donations.

The synagogue has faced many calamities. Roof falls, walls breaking down and many others. This synagogue stopped functioning as early as 1916, much before the mass immigration /exodus to Israel had begun. It became defunct as there were no more Bene Israels living in Ambepur. At that point in time, a muslim resident was entrusted with the duty of keeping the Tamid light burning though the synagogue was not in use. But then Soloman Dighorkar and his family took up the up-keep of the synagogue.

In 2014 when I visited the synagogue, I was told that the Dighorkar family had migrated to Israel 6 years back. Before they left, they sort of repaired the synagogue. Mr. Dighorkar handed over the synagogue to the Revdanda synagogue managing committee, who now try to look after it (Ambepur is 10 Km from Revdanda).

The synagogue today, 2014.

Inside the Hechal, a few relics, 2014.

A table and in its drawers a few kippas ,prayer books,,
candle stands etc. 2014.

George and me lighting candles in the synagogue, 2014.

The candles we lit, 2014.

Mr. Benjamin Waskar of Theronda, Revdanda tries to do as much as he can for the synagogue. He has hired a caretaker to look after the synagogue, its cleanliness etc.

When I visited it in 2014, it was in shambles. The caretaker does not bother to sweep it or clean it. There is no Tamid light, a few chandeliers are lying in a corner on the floor. There is only one table.

When you look at it from outside, it looks terrible, something like an old dilapidated typical village house on the verge of falling. No wonder it kept falling so many times. The well is to one side, it looks dirty and the well wall is in shambles. Also, the water is dirty. There is a lot of land surrounding the synagogue. Unfortunately no one to look after it.

When you go inside, there are no Sefer Torah. The few relics that I saw were,
- 2 glass hundies
- 2 white metal hundies
- 1 Hanukah
- Prayers books in the table drawers, old kippas, old curtains of the Hechal etc.

Recently about two years back i.e. 2012, a tree fell on the roof and completely destroyed it. Mr. Benjamin Waskar got it repaired at his own personal expence of Rs 40,000/-, of which one donor gave Rs 15,000/- while the rest was his contribution.

Recently one Mr. Daniel Cheulkar from Mumbai has bought a house in Ambepur, diagonally opposite to the synagogue. It is supposed to be a farm house.

It is my hope that he and his family will look after the synagogue.

VIII - Beth El Synagogue : Ashtami (Roha Taluka).

The name of the means 'House of God'.

This synagogue was built in 1882, but closed since a date I have not been able to ascertain. It was dedicated on Shavouth, the feast of the Pentacost.

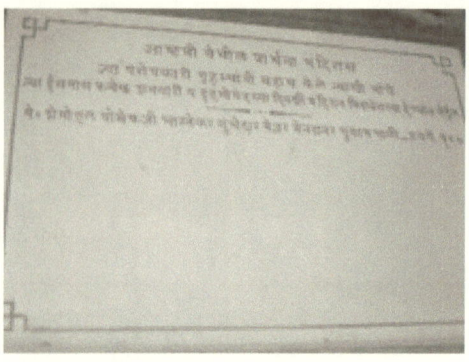

Plaque out side the synagogue, 2014.

Name of the synagogue above the
entrance which we found, 2014.

Outside view in 2014, George and me.

Initially the building was a simple village type house with a tiled roof and a latticework enclosed veranda. Unfortunately, the synagogue stopped functioning in the latter part of the nineteenth century, probably because not many Jews were left in Ashtami or there was no one to say the prayers. The exact date of closure and the reason for the closure is not known.

I remember visiting this synagogue as a child, when I was perhaps less than 10 years old, that was somewhere around the early 1950s. The synagogue reminded me as something more like a hut when looked at from outside, tiny, nothing much really. For Friday prayers, as I remember, we sat on mats, gents on one side, ladies to the other. It is now more than 100 years old. At the time of its glory, 15 – 20 families lived in Ashtami. It was handed over by David Ashtamkar in 1994 to the Zilla Parishad who are now running a school there.

In 2014 when I visited it, there was a coconut vendor standing just outside the school gate. He came forward and started talking to me. He asked me if I was a Yehudi and when I told him in the affirmative, he said that there is some lettering behind the photograph of Saraswati, the Goddess of learning, which was hanging just inside the entrance. I took the permission of the Principal of the school. The coconut vendor was so enthusiastic that he immediately climbed up, took down the photograph and began scraping the white wash that had been recently applied to the wall.

After some vigorous scraping, sure enough it revealed the name of the synagogue in Hebrew, BETH EL. It was just amazing, we all just stood there and kept looking at it. After some time, I went and requested the Principal to leave the name of the synagogue as it is and not cover it. He just looked at me and said nothing neither yes or no, so I repeated my request but again he said nothing. There was no chance that he could not have understood me, for I spoke in Marathi.

The name was just above the entrance door which leads to a small room with benches as in a class room. On the left side there was another classroom and on the right the Principal's office. The entrance to all these three rooms was from a veranda, which had trelliswork around it.

There is a well to the back the synagogue, which is pretty big. There is a wall built around it, short of the synagogue. The well and the land around the synagogue look as if they are left unclaimed. The saddest part according to me is that the school is named Chintamani Rao Pense School. Who gave this name and why, the principal could not tell me he probably did not want to tell me. The compound wall around the synagogue is partially destroyed. The well is covered with foliage. It is to the back of the synagogue where the locals told us people used to wash their hands and feet before entering the synagogue. There is quite a lot of land around the synagogue looking sad and unkept

I requested the Principal to retain the relics and the name of the synagogue as many Jews may come to visit the synagogue.

Translation

For Ashtami synagogue, all donor names will be displayed and they will be given Mish Baraka on Saturdays and festivals, Shri Samuel Yosefji Bhastekar.

IX - Shaar Ha Tefila Synagogue :
Mhasla, Mhasla Mahel

Address: Mhasla Bazaar Peth.

The name of the synagogue means 'Gates of Prayer'.

View from outside in 2000.

George before the closed entrance of the synagogue in 2000.

This synagogue was built in1863 and established in 1886. It was rebuilt in 1921. The synagogue was rebuilt by voluntary contributions and was dedicated on Monday 26th February 1921.

When I first visited the synagogue in 2000, we could not get the key to open it. It was disappointing. I was told that it was looked after by Moses Aptekar, who lives in Mumbai, and apparently looks after the cleanliness of the synagogue and also keeps the Tamid light burning.

Looking through the broken windowpanes during that visit, both the inside and outside of the synagogue were very dirty, there was no Tamid light as far as we could see.

In the old days, the community of Mhasla had services in a prayer hall. As the congregation grew, Khan Bahadur Shalom B Israel requested the ruler of Janjira, who generously allotted land and approved the construction of a prayer hall.

This prayer hall was used for 14 years. As requirements grew and the congregation increased in numbers, request for land extension was made, which was granted and the synagogue was built in 1863, which was a more solid structure and was then dedicated in 1886. There was a sizable community initially, which reduced as many moved to Bombay for economic reasons. With Israel's independence many moved to Israel and settled there.

The synagogue was rebuilt in 1921 by voluntary contributions and was rededicated on 26th February 1921. The ladies gallery was built in 1950.

My visit in 2014 was again futile, as once again we did not get to see the synagogue because we could not get the keys to the synagogue.

Today, no Jews are left in Mhasla. The synagogue is being looked after by remote control by Mr. Abraham Reuben Galsurkar, Mr. Shalom R Galsurkar, Mr. Binyamin R Garsulkar and Mr Jacob Abraham. Although no prayers are being said, occasionally I believe, they do go there and say the prayers. The Tamid light is not lit on a regular basis. When I visited in 2000 and 2002, it was pretty dirty, no Tamid light and there was grass growing wild all around.

I got the opportunity to visit the synagogue, when the Galsurkar family decided to celebrate the 120th anniversary of the synagogue on 1st March 2015. Although it was raining heavily, unusual for rains at that time of the year, the enthusiasm was palpable. People had come from all over, Mumbai, Thane, Pune, few guests I believe had also come from Israel, although personally I did not meet anyone. In all there were about a 100 guests.

At the 120 years anniversary celebrations, 2015

The entrance, 2015.

Exterior of the
synagogue, 2014.

The passage with
the entrance, 2015.

A marble tablet with the name of the synagogue above
the entrance, 2015.

The Ner Tamid and the door of the Hechal
with flower decorations, 2015.

That's me to the right, Moshe to the left, with the Teba in the background
before the start of the ceremonies, 2015

The woman's gallery seen from inside the synagogue, 2015.

Sefer Torahs inside the Hechal, 2015.

Oil lamps inside the synagogue, 2015.

The synagogue is quite big compared to the other Konkan synagogues and it has a lot of space inside the compound. The entrance, just like many synagogues in the Konkan, was in the main market area with a lot of hustle and bustle around. However, once you enter, it is quiet and peaceful .The entrance leads to a passage, which is actually through a building which is one storied and it sort of divides it into two halves. Coming out of the passage, which is about 10 feet or so, it opens into a space and in front of it is the synagogue entrance.

As you enter the passage, on the right, it seems as if there is a big hall, which I presume was for small functions, such as Brits, Marriages, Mehendi ceremony, Bar Mitzvah etc.To the left is the

129

office with a staircase on the side going up to the ladies gallery. There were also several doors, which were locked and which I presume lead to rooms where people could stay during marriages, visits etc.

They had made good arrangements for breakfast and lunch. The rains were playing spoilsport and the shamiana and outside decorations were totally ruined, to be specific, totally drenched. The flower arrangements and the decorations inside the synagogue were good and gave a really festive atmosphere. The synagogue was painted, clean and well done up.

There was a well at the back that was all covered up. There was a lot of land behind and on the side of the synagogue where the shamiana was put up. Right at the back and on one side, they had built a modern day toilet which was quite clean. At the entrance to the synagogue itself, there was a small wash basin where one could wash their hands before entering the synagogue, keeping up with the traditions of the Konkan area. To the side of the wash basin there is a door, beyond it there was a washing/bathing area.

X - Talekhar Synagogue in post Chordia, Talekhar – Murud Mahal.

This Synagogue was named after the village. It was built either in 1870 or 1892. But evidence shows that this synagogue was built in 1893 by Haeem Samuel Penkar. This synagogue did not function for long. It was closed around about the early 1900s, as there were no Bene Israels left in Talekhar. Most migrated to Mumbai and other parts of India. Bene Israels who resided in the surrounding villages such as Chorde, Chandgaon, Chanera, Kokban, Mhapua, Parankar, Sarsoli, Shirgaon and Tadgaon attended services in this synagogue.

Two stones, one indicating the presence of a synagogue which was demolished, for, as indicated on the second stone, the construction of a school.

I met Ezekiel Samuel Chordekar in 2000. His sister Diana Jonah Rohekar, who lives in Pune, gave me more information than her brother. Ezekiel Samuel Chordekar is the only Bene Israel living in Talekhar and now as of 2014, he too has migrated to Israel.

Their father Samuel Benjamin Chordekar, was the sarpanch of the village and also the Headmaster / Principal of the school. In the old days, there were 20 – 25 families living in Talekhar in extreme poverty, as they were loan ridden. Samuel Benjamin Chordekar as the sarpanch helped them migrate to Israel in 1965. He himself died around about 1985. At that point in time, only 2 families were left, one of Ezekiel Samuel Chordekar and another Pesha Chordekar.

Before his death, Samuel Benjamin Chordekar sent the Teba, hundies etc. to the Ambepur synagogue where we saw them lying on the floor in a corner against the wall, dirty and covered in cobwebs. He sent the benches, tables, Teba etc. to the Revdanda synagogue and the synagogue itself, he handed over to the Gram Panchayat.

Immediately after his death, a Ganapati idol was placed inside the synagogue, to which both the remaining Bene Israel families objected, they informed the police and with their help got the idol removed immediately.

The son Ezekiel Samuel Chordekar, whom I met during my visit in 2000, told me that a few years after his father handed over the synagogue to the Gram Panchayat, the synagogue building was demolished and when I saw it in 2000, they were building a school there.

There is now only one plaque left on the grounds which indicates where the synagogue was. The wordings though on the plaque are not very clear.

XI - Or Le Synagogue : Nandgaon

The name of the synagogue means "The Light". When this synagogue was built, it was in Janjira State, but now it is in the Alibagh Taluka.

The synagogue as seen from the gate in better times, 1985.

Marble plaque above the entrance with the name of the synagogue in Hebrew and Marathi, 2000

Teba with the Hechal in the background, 2000.

View from the gate, 2000

George and Moshe on the Teba, 2005.

It was built in 1896, rebuilt in 1945 and renovated in 1963. However, there is a lot of discrepancies regarding the dates. As of today, i.e. 2014, only one family is left, where there were about 50 families in Nandgaon and 15 in Usroli, which is 3 km away and whose families attended services in the Nandgaon synagogue.

The story goes that in 1896 pensioner Havaldar Moses Malyankar presented a plot of land to the Bene Israel community of Nandgaon for building a synagogue. Nothing was built for several years. A makeshift hut was built only in 1950 and it was built of mud. This required a lot of maintenance, so in 1958 after a jagran they demolished the mud structure and built a new synagogue with bricks and cement in its place and in February 1967, it was dedicated and named with a lot of pomp and ceremony. A malida was also said on the occasion.

As said earlier, Nandgaon was a usual village of the Konkan with more than 50 families living there initially, till about 1960s. Since then, exactly when not known, no prayers were being said in the synagogue and that is the state even today.

The upkeep of the synagogue however was in the hands of Menashe Benjamin Cheulkar. Since 1980, only his family is left in Nandgaon. Till he was alive, he looked after the welfare of the synagogue, he kept it neat and clean to the best of his ability. His family even today is doing quite well financially and are pretty wealthy. They own a lot of land with wadas, wadis and have a well paying transport business. At their residence they still have the old oil pressing machine which was pulled by bullocks. Although it is no longer in use, it is still quite an attraction.

In 2000, when I visited the synagogue it was well kept and the family was cordial towards visitors. The old man died in 2001 and thus began the decline of the synagogue. In 2005 when I visited, the sons as well as their mother made a lot of excuses, basically they did not want to open the synagogue. I volunteered to open it myself, close it and return the keys to them but they refused. I could understand their problem, visitors all the time, open and close the synagogue, and answer all the questions, maybe the same questions over and over, all the time. But visitors require just a little bit of courtesy that's all, anyway---

George and me at the entrance, 2014.

In 2014, when I visited, we went a little before sunset and although it was not completely dark, it was getting dark. One of the sons-in-law was there and he volunteered to open the synagogue for us. We got a shock. In the synagogue there was no electricity, as the electricity board had cut it because the electricity bills were not paid. What a shame really. We had one torch with us, so we tried to see the synagogue the best we could with that one torch. The saddest part was that the synagogue was filthy and it was stinking. We could make out that it was the toilet stink.

With the excuse of wanting to go to the toilet, which I actually wanted to see, I asked where the toilets were. Another shock awaited me.

The toilets were to the right side of the synagogue itself, while facing the Hechal. Very very unusual! For no synagogues have attached toilets in the same building as the synagogue, with the entrance door of the toilets in the main synagogue itself. At least I had never seen such a thing and I have visited many synagogues. I felt ashamed and disgusted.

However, when I entered through the door, there was a lot of space with the toilets to the end, at the level of the Hechal. I was shocked to see the state the toilets were in. The stench was unbearable and I quickly walked out. I could not even wait to take a picture.

I was told that although the other siblings have donated sufficient money and kept it in the bank for use of the synagogue, the two boys still living there are just not bothered or interested. One is a drunkard who has had 2 failed marriages. The other and the mother don't care at all. Such a pity, I only hope and pray that some sense prevails and they could hire help and improve things. Such a beautiful synagogue ---just going to the dogs.

XII - Bene Israel Synagogue - Talley Ghosale

This synagogue was built in 1862, but it is closed since a date that I have not been able to ascertain.

People in the village pointed out a small building which they said was the synagogue, which later on when most of the Bene Israels of that village left, was handed over to the Zilla Parishad who now run a Bal Wadi (kindergarten) there.

George with the caretaker of the graveyard, Chavan who showed us the synagogue site as well as the graveyard, 2014.

George at the entrance, 2014.

When we went to that house, there was a Bal wadi board where the synagogue should have been. But that day the school was not in session. We looked around from the outside at the interiors, but we could not see anything. The wood paneling was on the inside so we could not see if there was a mezuzah on the door-post as the door was closed. Also, there was no name at the entrance or above the door. The surrounding area was presumably the compound of the synagogue. We looked carefully all over the grounds of the compound, but there were no plaques, symbols or anything like a foundation stone or something, no Jewish symbols to indicate that there was a synagogue here previously. Unfortunately we did not find anything. However, to the back and on one side there was a well which was covered by branches of trees, but when we looked inside, the well seemed deep. The presence of a well to one side and a lot of surrounding land, very typical of all the synagogues in the Konkan, speaks for itself. In my opinion, it was definitely the synagogue of Talley Ghosale.

I asked a number of villagers, especially the older generation, many of whom vouched that, that was the synagogue where the Jews of not only that village but also from the surrounding villages prayed.

We met one person who came forward to talk to us. His name was Chavan Hasya Tulve. He was young and hence did not know much about the synagogue, but he had heard from the elders of his own family and the other villagers too, that it was indeed the Jewish synagogue where they prayed and after they all left, they handed over the synagogue property to the Zilla Parishad, who have been running a Bal Wadi there.

He also told us that he had the key to the graveyard which was quite close to the synagogue. So we trooped there. The graveyard was kept quite clean, everything including the graves were clean and washed. There was a newly built grave there and we asked him about it. According to him, one Mr. Malyankar from Israel had come there and built a grave for his aunt who had died in the early 1990s.

One source mentioned that there were about 30 houses / families living there and they had only a prayer hall, where they said all their prayers, which was the house where there is a Bal Wadi now. It is plain rationalizing that probably because it was not a synagogue, just a prayer hall, there was no Hechal, no tamid light, no hundies. Again rationalizing that this would probably explain why we did not find any plaques or Jewish symbols either inside or in the surrounding areas except for the well. Just plain conjecture, because the other prayer halls had all the Jewish symbols.

XIII - Beth El Synagogue Panvel :
The name of the synagogue means 'House Of God'.

Outer wall and entrance

Address : Mirchi Galli, Mahatma Gandhi Road,
Panvel - 410206.

The credit for the building of this synagogue also goes to late Hacham Shellomo Salem Shurrabi, not only for its establishment but also to impress on the people the love of God. Previous to the building of the synagogue, a prayer hall was opened, at first at the residence of Aaron Elijah Nawgaonkar and subsequently at the residence of Joseph David Sankar, who was generous enough to donate his own house and grounds on which the Panvel's Beth El synagogue was built in 1849. A Torah scroll was gifted by the Karachi synagogue to the Panvel synagogue as the Presidents of both the synagogues were related.

The Bene Israels of Panvel in addition to the usual trades of the Bene Israels of the Konkan, were also engaged in small-scale cottage industries. Some of them owned tongas (horse-drawn carriages) and some owned motor-buses for ferrying passengers. Several Bene Israels from Panvel have been Chairman or members of the Panvel municipal committee, or local boards.

Here also the spirit of jealousy was prevalent and displayed now and then by the members, which gave rise to two factions within the synagogue, although often they united during the prayers. though, not always. The members were constantly feuding with each other and I found that this situation exists even today.

A small passage leading to the entrance of the synagogue, 2000.

Outside of the synagogue 2006

The interiors 2016

A Renovated Hechal.

This is one of the oldest synagogues in Raigad District. It was built in 1849 by means of subscriptions from the Bene Isreals in India and was dedicated on 17th May 1849 on Shavouth. This synagogue has 9 special significances of its own.

1) The torah was given to Moshe on Shavouth and this synagogue was dedicated on Shavouth (member's opinions).

2) A whole night's vigil called Jagran with prayers is held on Shavouth. On one such occasion, after the prayers were over and the synagogue was locked, outside the synagogue

there were people sitting and they said that they could hear someone praying loudly. They told this to the members of the synagogue. I believe this has happened on several occasions.

3) In every synagogue there are 2 decorated chairs kept which are used during the Brit. In the Panvel synagogue, there are 3 chairs. There is a belief that several of our ancestors nearly 100 years ago, some say 120 years ago or even 150 years ago, have seen the prophet Elijah sit on one of those chairs. So as a practice, one chair is always kept there for him, called The Eliyahu Hannavi chair. Where it is placed has been the same since the inception of the synagogue i.e. from 17th May 1849. The position of the chair is important and is of great significance. The community has said the Eliyahu Hanavi prayers at the same spot and kept its sanctity. That is why vows taken there are always fulfilled, they believe, after which people come back and say the malida prayers.

4) There are 2 pillars at the entrance. And at the entrance, it is written in Hebrew that only those can enter who believe in God and have a pure mind, soul and body. How they judge that, I would certainly like to know.

5) It is only in the Panvel synagogue till about 10 to 15 years back that the 'Sukkah' was always built in front of the synagogue. The belief was that it was told in the scriptures that the 'Sukkah' had to be built at the entrance. The three sides closed, one side open in front, so entry into the synagogue becomes difficult. The reason for this is not known. Later on, good sense prevailed as the members found it difficult to enter the synagogue during Succoth. Now they build it to one side like the other synagogues.

6) According to some, it is the only synagogue facing north west i.e. towards Jerusalem, which is very important and significant. Prayers said there go straight to Jerusalem. WOW! Great.

7) Sanctity of the synagogue is observed strictly as far as the Hechal and Torah are concerned. So also the old customs

and traditions are observed ---even if they are out dated.

8) Power comes from heaven to the Torah, so the belief is that it is a joint effort of God and the Torah to bless the community. Why specifically only this synagogue and not the others?

9) It is supposed to be the most vibrant synagogue. Frankly, in what way I can't understand.

Thus it is believed by many that whatever vows are taken, maybe for a child, for an illness, for health reasons whatever, these vows once fulfilled, the persons concerned visit the synagogue, offer thanksgiving prayers and say the Malida.

The synagogue celebrated its 120th anniversary on Sunday 15th February 1920. It is a modest structure, close to the main square of the town.

One Mr. Reuben Kamarlekar a Bene Israel settled in Israel for several years stayed in Panvel for months at a stretch and supervised the renovation work of the synagogue from 1994 to 1995. He collected donations from various people in Israel, added his own contribution, came to India, visited Rajasthan where he bought marble slabs for the walls and flooring of the synagogue. He bought Dholpuri stone slabs for the wall outside the synagogue. Then he came to Panvel, stayed for more than 6 months and supervised the workers every day for the whole day and got the work done. He must have got the workers from Rajasthan, for they have done an excellent job. It withstood the force of the deluge in 2005. I am sure the members of the Panvel synagogue must be really grateful to him.

The present treasurer of the synagogue committee Yaffa Kolatkar is Mr. Reuben Kamarlekar's sister. She told me that he died in Israel in 2013.

On 26th July 2005, there were heavy rains and a cloud burst in the vicinity of the synagogue, with flooding all over the Raigad district. Of all the synagogues in Mumbai and Raigad, the Beth El synagogue of Panvel was the worst hit. Water had accumulated in the synagogue right up to the ladies gallery.

At the time the water entered the synagogue and was rising, two people were in the synagogue, the chazan and one Mr. Mapgaonkar, the administrative head. They said that the speed at which the water was rising was so scary that they rushed out and went to a nearby building and hid in the loft for 48 hours. It was a harrowing experience especially for Mr. Mapgaonkar, as he is a polio victim.

After the deluge, above and below.

The damaged Sefer Torah after the deluge, 2005.

The water level slowly started falling after 24 -36 hours. They waited till it was 48 hours and then opened the synagogue. They found the Teba, which was fixed to the flooring by solid cement, had moved and was now at an angle. Also the Hechal, which houses the Sefer Torahs and is made of solid oak, had pitched forward and was resting on the Ner Tamid light. The upper chamber of the Hechal housed 15 Sefer Torahs, one of which was brand new and had just been donated to the synagogue.

The lower chamber had all the linen required for the various festivals and various occassions, curtains, table cloths, sheets, hamotzi covers etc. The water had everything soaking wet and smelly and it required a gargantuan effort of several people to lift and straighten the Hechal. With all this damage, one can imagine what must have been the force and fury of the water.

When the Bene Israel community of Panvel got together, they found that the synagogue floor was covered with one foot of silt, in some places it was even one and a half feet of mud, silt and debris. All the members got together to clean the synagogue. It took them 8 days of working from morning to night to clear the debris. Some women cooked meals outside the synagogue, so they all ate together there itself and did not have to go home. Everything was destroyed, the books, Jewish symbols, including the Sefer Torahs, which had to be buried after consultations with various Rabbis and religious heads. The Sefer Torahs were buried in the compound of the synagogue after the requisite prayers were said.

The first Sabbath after the deluge, no prayers were said in the synagogue. The synagogue sent out a desperate plea for help. The first synagogue to respond was the Succath Shelomo synagogue (SSS) Pune where Dr. George Judah was the President. He took two Sefes Torahs, one Parasha and one Haftara and loaned them to the Panvel synagogue. In addition, the SSS donated several books, linen, wine cups etc. All these were carried to the Panvel synagogue, the first Sunday after the first Sabbath when prayers were not said in the synagogue. They were personally carried by Dr George Judah in his own car along with his wife, yours truly, Dr Irene Judah and their son Akiv. I personally donated several books, Sabbath and Havdalah glasses, Hamotzi covers and tablecloths to the synagogue.

George and Akiv with the Sefer Torah outside the synagogue.

Putting the Sefer Torah
into the Hechal.

Two Sefer Torahs given to the
synagogue on loan by the
Succath Shelomo Synagogue
Pune where George was
the President at that time.

The following Sunday, one more Haftara Sefer was loaned by the old synagogue of Mumbai - the Shaarei Rahamim synagogue. One Sefer was donated by a well-wisher from Israel and it was brought to the Beth El synagogue on 8th September 2005. AC's were donated and installed by Romiel Moses Bhonkar, my daughter-in-law Hannah's brother, after the deluge. The synagogue was also painted and a few cursory repairs were also carried out.

The synagogue roof has also been also repaired lately. As of now, the synagogue is all spruced up and looks really good. They try to have the Sabbath prayers both on Friday evening and Saturday morning but very often there is no minyan. On festivals the synagogue is full.

A couple of times I have attended Rosh Hashanah prayers in this synagogue, I am always impressed with the spirit of the people. After the morning prayers, everybody sits in the open space outside the synagogue. Every family, obviously the women of the family, bring along whatever sweet has been prepared for the festival and it is shared by everyone, guests included, who may not have brought anything. The synagogue contributes some dishes from their side. There is a tremendous feeling of togetherness and I must say, it is very impressive. They also give you a carry bag, so if you cannot finish all the eats, you can carry them home. I found this spirit of Rosh Hashana really inspiring.

XIV - Chandgaon - Roha Taluka.

Chandgaon lies between Roha and Revdanda. It had a sizable number of families, about 10 to 12. I am not sure if they had a synagogue or a prayer hall.

Later on they went to Nhave synagogue or any other synagogue in the surrounding villages like Pezari, Nowgaon etc. I did not find any specific criteria or information about their religious services.

XV - Roha - Roha Taluka.

There was quite a sizable population of Bene Israels in Roha. Initially, I believe, they conducted prayers in their respective homes. Then they built a huge hall where they had their prayers. I am not sure if it was a synagogue or a prayer hall, and when was it built and when was it consecrated and what was it named. Whatever, it was handed over to the Rotary club, but when exactly, is again not known.

I saw it in 1998 on one of my trips. It was just an empty huge hall, pretty big compared to all the other synagogues and prayer halls that I had seen in the Konkan area. I did not find any Jewish relics there such as a Mezuza, Hechal, Teba, prayer books, kippas etc. The caretaker of that place could not give me any details except that it was a place where the Jews had their prayers. When that stopped, he did not know. They had handed it over to the rotary club, where the Rotarians held their meetings. I tried to contact some Rotarians of that area but they too could not provide any information.

Some Jews that I spoke to told me that prayers stopped in the Roha synagogue when the number of Jews reduced and they had no one to say the prayers in the synagogue, or even get someone to say the prayers for them although they were willing to pay. So they said the Sabbath prayers at their respective homes and for the festivals, many went to Ashtami, which was just across the river or they went to the other neighboring villages wherever there was a synagogue.

Some others told me that because of the mass migration to Israel, prayers stopped, the exact year is not known and why they handed over the synagogue to the Rotary club is also not known.

XVI - Palli Synagogue

Initially there were about 20 families in Palli. A prayer hall was started in 1957 or 1958, stopped after 2 years, for what reason the lady of the house could not tell. Most probably some dispute. The prayers were restarted and continued for 2 more years.

The prayer hall where the prayers were said was at the residence of Mr. Jacob Palkar. He had kept one big room solely for the purpose of prayers. Then, the prayers stopped about 30 years back. They then restarted and continued for 4 years. Since 1968 no prayers are being said in Palli. Many of the Jews now go elsewhere either to Pen, Panvel or any other synagogue.

The community in Palli were very observant and strict. On Sabbath, they closed the oil press shop. Now most of the members have gone to Israel, one family is in Panvel and I spoke to the lady of the house.

Mr. Jacob Palkar had a restaurant 'Palkar Hotel' and above that was the prayer hall, where in 1957 or 1958 prayers were started. Then they stopped, resumed and again stopped. Since 1968 no prayers are being said there. One of the reasons, I surmised was that right now only 5 families are left in Palli and whenever required they take the services of Mr. Benjamin Waskar of Revdanda.

XVII - Chordai Synagogue in Chordai.

Chordai is the name of the village, the name of the synagogue is not known or probably it was named after the place itself.

Ezekiel Chordekar had handed over the synagogue to the Zilla Parishad in 2000, who demolished the building and are now building a school on that land.

The synagogue was built by Abraham Chordekar and his brother Ezekiel Chordekar, the year is not known. At that point in time there were about 25 families in Chordai. Most went to Israel by 1965, following which only 2 families remained. In 2000 when I visited there was only one person living there, who on my subsequent visit in 2014 we could not trace. His name is also Ezekiel Chordekar.

When I visited the site of the synagogue building in 2000 and spoke to the only Jew left in Chordai, who is the son of Ezekiel Chordekar, he told me about the synagogue and also the following. When the synagogue building was handed over to the Zilla Parishad, the wooden furniture such as the benches, teba, tables etc. were handed over to some local body, who when all the Jews left burnt all the wooden furniture. That's that.

The utensils, hundies and other Jewish relics were donated to the old synagogue in Mumbai.

In 2014 when we went there, we could not find him or exactly where the synagogue stood. Where we thought the synagogue should have been, there was no school.

XVIII - Murud

There were a number of Bene Israels living and working in the fort and palace of Murud on the administrative side, looking after the finances and also in the fighting force. The Nawab of Murud gave a piece of land for the purpose of building a synagogue.

However, the synagogue was not built immediately, in fact it was not built for a very long time; because of which, over the years , the land was encroached on by the other local population.

The congregation of Murud went to Talla for prayers. There is however a graveyard there to this day, with a well built boundary wall. Graves of some Bene Israels like Dr Abraham Kolatkar are there. I am not aware who these people were. Also I believe the Mashilkars of Murud and one Aaron Nagavkar were actors in Marathi plays. Also I believe his son Levi acted in films.

XIX - Janjira

Like Murud, many of the Bene Israels in Janjira worked for Royalty and likewise the Nawab of Janjira had given them a plot of land to build a synagogue. However, I believe that plot of land was also for a school and one Mr. Ashtamkar started a Marathi school there, which exists till today.

Although there are no plaques or Jewish relics to indicate the existence of a synagogue or a prayer hall, there are a number of plaques in the fort indicative of the presence of the Bene Israels in the fort in important positions. Their names exist on the various boards still in existence in the Janjira Fort.

XX - Pezari

There was a sizable community of Bene Israels in Pezari. The locals told me about their existence but could not give me any information about the existence of a place where they used to say their prayers. Right now there is no Bene Israel family living in Pezari and the Bene Israels from the surrounding areas could not give me any information but said that they had heard of the existence of either a synagogue or a prayer hall, where exactly and at what point in time, they could not tell me.

XXI - Navgaon

There is definite existence of a synagogue / prayer hall, but no other details are known.

Existence of twelve more synagogues is definitely known but I could not get any more details.

XXII - Ghosali

XXIII - Virjoli

XXIV - Shrivardhan

XXV - Mahad

XXVI - Rajpuri

XXVII - Kihim

XXVIII - Thal

XXIX - Akshi

XXX - Nagoan

XXXI - Saswane

XXXII - Dighordy

XXXIII - Nowgaon

Many more villages had either prayer halls or synagogues but no details are available or rather I should say that I could not gather any details.

❑ ❑ ❑

Bibliography

1) The History of the Bene Israels of India by Haeem Samuel Kehimkar. He lived between 1830 and 1908. He died at the age of 78. His book was published 40 years after his death. He was the first one to document in writing the history of the Bene Israels.

2) India's Bene Israels by Shirley Bery Isenberg.

3) Study of Indian Jewish Identity by Nathan Katz.

4) Jews of India by M. D. Japheth.

5) Jews of India by Benjamin J Israel.

6) The Jews of India by the Jewish Welfare Association New Delhi

❑ ❑ ❑

About the Author

Dr Irene Judah has retired from the Armed Forces Medical College. She continued working after retirement till last year. She always wanted to write and document about the Bene Israels and their ancestors. Her interest in the synagogues has been present since her childhood. Documenting and writing about them is of prime importance to her right now.